T0357573

ANTON CHEKHOV

SELECTED SHORT STORIES

ANTON CHEKHOV

SELECTED SHORT STORIES

SIRIUS

SIRIUS

This edition published in 2024 by Sirius Publishing, a division of
Arcturus Publishing Limited,
26/27 Bickels Yard, 151–153 Bermondsey Street,
London SE1 3HA

ISBN: 978-1-3988-5118-4
AD006015UK

Printed in China

Contents

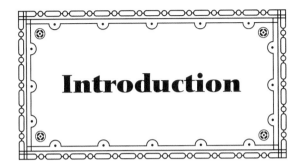

Introduction

Anton Chekhov (1860–1904) was born in the small port town of Taganrov, on the Sea of Azov in southern Russia. His father, Pavel, was a bully and a despot who ran a grocery shop and acted as director of the local church choir. His mother, Yevgeniya, managed the household and looked after their six children, telling them stories of her experiences of travelling with her father who was a mercer.

When Pavel was declared bankrupt in 1876, the family moved to Moscow, where Chekhov's two older brothers, Alexander and Nikolai, were at university. Chekhov was left in Taganrov to continue his education and oversee the sale of the family's possessions. He took up work as a private tutor and began his writing career by selling pieces to newspapers. Once he had finished his education, Chekhov joined the rest of his family in Moscow, having also gained a place at the I. M. Sechenov First Moscow State Medical University in 1879.

Drawing on the characters of his family as well as the local street life, Chekhov continued with his writing, using the income from his work to help pay his tuition fees and support his family, who had come to rely on him. Although Chekhov qualified as a doctor in 1884, his success was tainted by the fact that he exhibited the first signs of tuberculosis, coughing up blood in a series of attacks which grew worse over the next two years. Stubbornly, he refused to seek medical advice, not wanting to be examined by his colleagues.

Spending his time helping the poor, it was his writing that provided Chekhov with a serious income. In 1886, the millionaire Alexei Suvorin asked him to write for his newspaper, *Novoye Vremya* (*New Times*). Chekhov's work attracted attention, and he produced a volume of short stories, *At Dusk*, that won him the Pushkin Prize in 1888. Despite his ill health, Chekhov diversified his work, writing a novella, *The Steppe*, and then the first of his plays, *Ivanov*, which was critically well received. Chekhov was not enamoured of writing for the stage, but *Ivanov* and his subsequent plays – *The Seagull*, *Uncle Vanya*, *The Three Sisters* and *The Cherry Orchard* – helped to revolutionise playwriting and performing through their focus on expressing how people really thought and spoke.

When his brother Nikolai died of tuberculosis in 1889, Chekhov became severely depressed. His younger brother, Mikhail, was conducting research in prisons and this prompted Chekhov to focus on the subject of prison reform. In 1890, he spent three months on Sakhalin Island interviewing convicts as part of a census. The experience provided a great store of inspiration for his writing.

In 1897, Chekhov suffered a severe lung haemorrhage and the doctors confirmed that he did have tuberculosis. They advised him to slow down, so he built a villa near Yalta, and moved in with his family. He also quietly married one of his protégées, Olga Knipper, in 1901. Three years later, though, the tuberculosis finally took its toll, and Anton Chekhov died on 15 July 1904 while staying in the German spa town of Badenweiler.

Chekhov left a prolific body of work, including plays, short stories, newspaper articles, one novel and five novellas. Over successive generations, his work has fallen in and out of favour, but Leo Tolstoy, whom Chekhov knew, was a huge admirer of his short stories, and many of those collected here were considered by Tolstoy to be among Chekhov's best work. Chekhov's legacy can be seen across the world of literature: George Bernard Shaw, James Joyce and Virginia Woolf were all influenced by his style, as were playwrights such as Tennessee Williams and Shimizu Kunio. While Chekhov avoided controversial political and philosophical statements, he remains one of the greatest and wittiest observers of everyday life.

At the Barber's

Morning. It is not yet seven o'clock, but Makar Kuzmitch Blyostken's shop is already open. The barber himself, an unwashed, greasy, but foppishly dressed youth of three and twenty, is busy clearing up; there is really nothing to be cleared away, but he is perspiring with his exertions. In one place he polishes with a rag, in another he scrapes with his finger or catches a bug and brushes it off the wall.

The barber's shop is small, narrow, and unclean. The log walls are hung with paper suggestive of a cabman's faded shirt. Between the two dingy, perspiring windows there is a thin, creaking, rickety door, above it, green from the damp, a bell which trembles and gives a sickly ring of itself without provocation. Glance into the looking-glass which hangs on one of the walls, and it distorts your countenance in all directions in the most merciless way! The shaving and haircutting is done before this looking-glass. On the little table, as greasy and unwashed as Makar Kuzmitch himself, there is everything: combs, scissors, razors, a ha'porth of wax for the moustache, a ha'porth of powder, a ha'porth of much watered eau de Cologne, and indeed the whole barber's shop is not worth more than fifteen kopecks.

There is a squeaking sound from the invalid bell and an elderly man in a tanned sheepskin and high felt over-boots walks into the shop. His head and neck are wrapped in a woman's shawl.

This is Erast Ivanitch Yagodov, Makar Kuzmitch's godfather. At one time he served as a watchman in the Consistory, now he lives near the Red Pond and works as a locksmith.

'Makarushka, good-day, dear boy!' he says to Makar Kuzmitch, who is absorbed in tidying up.

They kiss each other. Yagodov drags his shawl off his head, crosses himself, and sits down.

'What a long way it is!' he says, sighing and clearing his throat. 'It's no joke! From the Red Pond to the Kaluga gate.'

'How are you?'

'In a poor way, my boy. I've had a fever.'

'You don't say so! Fever!'

'Yes, I have been in bed a month; I thought I should die. I had extreme unction. Now my hair's coming out. The doctor says I must be shaved. He says the hair will grow again strong. And so, I thought, I'll go to Makar. Better to a relation than to anyone else. He will do it better and he won't take anything for it. It's rather far, that's true, but what of it? It's a walk.'

'I'll do it with pleasure. Please sit down.'

With a scrape of his foot Makar Kuzmitch indicates a chair. Yagodov sits down and looks at himself in the glass and is apparently pleased with his reflection: the looking-glass displays a face awry, with Kalmuck lips, a broad, blunt nose, and eyes in the forehead. Makar Kuzmitch puts round his client's shoulders a white sheet with yellow spots on it, and begins snipping with the scissors.

'I'll shave you clean to the skin!' he says.

'To be sure. So that I may look like a Tartar, like a bomb. The hair will grow all the thicker.'

'How's auntie?'

'Pretty middling. The other day she went as midwife to the major's lady. They gave her a rouble.'

'Oh, indeed, a rouble. Hold your ear.'

'I am holding it… Mind you don't cut me. Oy, you hurt! You are pulling my hair.'

'That doesn't matter. We can't help that in our work. And how is Anna Erastovna?'

'My daughter? She is all right, she's skipping about. Last week on the Wednesday we betrothed her to Sheikin. Why didn't you come?'

The scissors cease snipping. Makar Kuzmitch drops his hands and asks in a fright:

'Who is betrothed?'

'Anna.'

'How's that? To whom?'

'To Sheikin. Prokofy Petrovitch. His aunt's a housekeeper in Zlatoustensky Lane. She is a nice woman. Naturally we are all delighted, thank God. The wedding will be in a week. Mind you come; we will have a good time.'

'But how's this, Erast Ivanitch?' says Makar Kuzmitch, pale, astonished, and shrugging his shoulders. 'It's… it's utterly impossible. Why, Anna Erastovna… why I… why, I cherished sentiments for her, I had intentions. How could it happen?'

'Why, we just went and betrothed her. He's a good fellow.'

Cold drops of perspiration come on the face of Makar Kuzmitch. He puts the scissors down on the table and begins rubbing his nose with his fist.

'I had intentions,' he says. 'It's impossible, Erast Ivanitch. I… I am in love with her and have made her the offer of my heart… And auntie promised. I have always respected you as though you were my father… I always cut your hair for nothing… I have always obliged you, and when my papa died you took the sofa and ten roubles in cash and have never given them back. Do you remember?'

'Remember! of course I do. Only, what sort of a match would you be, Makar? You are nothing of a match. You've neither money nor position, your trade's a paltry one.'

'And is Sheikin rich?'

'Sheikin is a member of a union. He has a thousand and a half lent on mortgage. So my boy… It's no good talking about it, the thing's done. There is no altering it, Makarushka. You must look out for another bride… The world is not so small. Come, cut away. Why are you stopping?'

Makar Kuzmitch is silent and remains motionless, then he takes a handkerchief out of his pocket and begins to cry.

'Come, what is it?' Erast Ivanitch comforts him. 'Give over. Fie, he is blubbering like a woman! You finish my head and then cry. Take up the scissors!'

Makar Kuzmitch takes up the scissors, stares vacantly at them for a minute, then drops them again on the table. His hands are shaking.

'I can't,' he says. 'I can't do it just now. I haven't the strength! I am a miserable man! And she is miserable! We loved each other, we had given each other our promise and we have been separated by unkind people without any pity. Go away, Erast Ivanitch! I can't bear the sight of you.'

'So I'll come tomorrow, Makarushka. You will finish me tomorrow.'

'Right.'

'You calm yourself and I will come to you early in the morning.'

Erast Ivanitch has half his head shaven to the skin and looks like a convict. It is awkward to be left with a head like that, but there is no help for it. He wraps his head in the shawl and walks out of the barber's shop. Left alone, Makar Kuzmitch sits down and goes on quietly weeping.

Early next morning Erast Ivanitch comes again.

'What do you want?' Makar Kuzmitch asks him coldly.

'Finish cutting my hair, Makarushka. There is half the head left to do.'

'Kindly give me the money in advance. I won't cut it for nothing.'

Without saying a word Erast Ivanitch goes out, and to this day his hair is long on one side of the head and short on the other. He regards it as extravagance to pay for having his hair cut and is waiting for the hair to grow of itself on the shaven side.

He danced at the wedding in that condition.

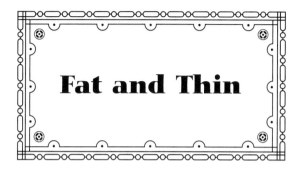

Fat and Thin

Two friends – one a fat man and the other a thin man – met at the Nikolaevsky station. The fat man had just dined in the station and his greasy lips shone like ripe cherries. He smelt of sherry and *fleur d'orange*. The thin man had just slipped out of the train and was laden with portmanteaus, bundles, and bandboxes. He smelt of ham and coffee grounds. A thin woman with a long chin, his wife, and a tall schoolboy with one eye screwed up came into view behind his back.

'Porfiry,' cried the fat man on seeing the thin man. 'Is it you? My dear fellow! How many summers, how many winters!'

'Holy saints!' cried the thin man in amazement. 'Misha! The friend of my childhood! Where have you dropped from?'

The friends kissed each other three times, and gazed at each other with eyes full of tears. Both were agreeably astounded.

'My dear boy!' began the thin man after the kissing. 'This is unexpected! This is a surprise! Come have a good look at me! Just as handsome as I used to be! Just as great a darling and a dandy! Good gracious me! Well, and how are you? Made your fortune? Married? I am married as you see… This is my wife Luise, her maiden name was Vantsenbach… of the Lutheran persuasion… And this is my son Nafanail, a schoolboy in the third class. This is the friend of my childhood, Nafanya. We were boys at school together!'

Nafanail thought a little and took off his cap.

'We were boys at school together,' the thin man went on. 'Do you remember how they used to tease you? You were nicknamed Herostratus because you burned a hole in a schoolbook with a cigarette, and I was nicknamed Ephialtes because I was fond of telling tales. Ho–ho!… we were children!… Don't be shy, Nafanya. Go nearer to him. And this is my wife, her maiden name was Vantsenbach, of the Lutheran persuasion…'

Nafanail thought a little and took refuge behind his father's back.

'Well, how are you doing my friend?' the fat man asked, looking enthusiastically at his friend. 'Are you in the service? What grade have you reached?'

'I am, dear boy! I have been a collegiate assessor for the last two years and I have the Stanislav. The salary is poor, but that's no great matter! The wife gives music lessons, and I go in for carving wooden cigarette cases in a private way. Capital cigarette cases! I sell them for a rouble each. If any one takes ten or more I make a reduction of course. We get along somehow. I served as a clerk, you know, and now I have been transferred here as a head clerk in the same department. I am going to serve here. And what about you? I bet you are a civil councillor by now? Eh?'

'No dear boy, go higher than that,' said the fat man. 'I have risen to privy councillor already… I have two stars.'

The thin man turned pale and rigid all at once, but soon his face twisted in all directions in the broadest smile; it seemed as though sparks were flashing from his face and eyes. He squirmed, he doubled together, crumpled up… His portmanteaus, bundles and cardboard boxes seemed to shrink and crumple up too… His wife's long chin grew longer still; Nafanail drew himself up to attention and fastened all the buttons of his uniform.

'Your Excellency, I… delighted! The friend, one may say, of childhood and to have turned into such a great man! He–he!'

'Come, come!' the fat man frowned. 'What's this tone for? You and I were friends as boys, and there is no need of this official obsequiousness!'

'Merciful heavens, your Excellency! What are you saying…?' sniggered the thin man, wriggling more than ever. 'Your Excellency's gracious attention is like refreshing manna… This, your Excellency, is my son Nafanail,… my wife Luise, a Lutheran in a certain sense.'

The fat man was about to make some protest, but the face of the thin man wore an expression of such reverence, sugariness, and mawkish respectfulness that the privy councillor was sickened. He turned away from the thin man, giving him his hand at parting.

The thin man pressed three fingers, bowed his whole body and sniggered like a Chinaman: 'He–he–he!' His wife smiled. Nafanail scraped with his foot and dropped his cap. All three were agreeably overwhelmed.

A Malefactor

An exceedingly lean little peasant, in a striped hempen shirt and patched drawers, stands facing the investigating magistrate. His face overgrown with hair and pitted with smallpox, and his eyes scarcely visible under thick, overhanging eyebrows have an expression of sullen moroseness. On his head there is a perfect mop of tangled, unkempt hair, which gives him an even more spider-like air of moroseness. He is barefooted.

'Denis Grigoryev!' the magistrate begins. 'Come nearer, and answer my questions. On the seventh of this July the railway watchman, Ivan Semyonovitch Akinfov, going along the line in the morning, found you at the hundred-and-forty-first mile engaged in unscrewing a nut by which the rails are made fast to the sleepers. Here it is, the nut!… With the aforesaid nut he detained you. Was that so?'

'Wha-at?'

'Was this all as Akinfov states?'

'To be sure, it was.'

'Very good; well, what were you unscrewing the nut for?'

'Wha-at?'

'Drop that "wha-at" and answer the question; what were you unscrewing the nut for?'

'If I hadn't wanted it I shouldn't have unscrewed it,' croaks Denis, looking at the ceiling.

'What did you want that nut for?'

'The nut? We make weights out of those nuts for our lines.'

'Who is "we"?'

'We, people… The Klimovo peasants, that is.'

'Listen, my man; don't play the idiot to me, but speak sensibly. It's no use telling lies here about weights!'

'I've never been a liar from a child, and now I'm telling lies…' mutters Denis, blinking. 'But can you do without a weight, your honour? If you put live bait or maggots on a hook, would it go to the bottom without a weight?… I am telling lies,' grins Denis… 'What the devil is the use of the worm if it swims on the surface! The perch and the pike and the eel-pout always go to the bottom, and a bait on the surface is only taken by a shillisper, not very often then, and there are no shillispers in our river… That fish likes plenty of room.'

'Why are you telling me about shillispers?'

'Wha-at? Why, you asked me yourself! The gentry catch fish that way too in our parts. The silliest little boy would not try to catch a fish without a weight. Of course anyone who did not understand might go to fish without a weight. There is no rule for a fool.'

'So you say you unscrewed this nut to make a weight for your fishing line out of it?'

'What else for? It wasn't to play knuckle-bones with!'

'But you might have taken lead, a bullet… a nail of some sort…'

'You don't pick up lead in the road, you have to buy it, and a nail's no good. You can't find anything better than a nut… It's heavy, and there's a hole in it.'

'He keeps pretending to be a fool! as though he'd been born yesterday or dropped from heaven! Don't you understand, you block-head, what unscrewing these nuts leads to? If the watchman had not noticed it the train might have run off the rails, people would have been killed – you would have killed people.'

'God forbid, your honour! What should I kill them for? Are we heathens or wicked people? Thank God, good gentlemen, we have lived all our lives without ever dreaming of such a thing… Save, and have mercy on us, Queen of Heaven!… What are you saying?'

'And what do you suppose railway accidents do come from? Unscrew two or three nuts and you have an accident.'

Denis grins, and screws up his eye at the magistrate incredulously.

'Why! how many years have we all in the village been unscrewing nuts, and the Lord has been merciful; and you talk of accidents, killing people. If I had carried away a rail or put a log across the line, say, then maybe it might have upset the train, but… pouf! a nut!'

'But you must understand that the nut holds the rail fast to the sleepers!'

'We understand that… We don't unscrew them all… we leave some… We don't do it thoughtlessly… we understand…'

Denis yawns and makes the sign of the cross over his mouth.

'Last year the train went off the rails here,' says the magistrate. 'Now I see why!'

'What do you say, your honour?'

'I am telling you that now I see why the train went off the rails last year… I understand!'

'That's what you are educated people for, to understand, you kind gentlemen. The Lord knows to whom to give understanding… Here you have reasoned how and what, but the watchman, a peasant like ourselves, with no understanding at all, catches one by the collar and hauls one along… You should reason first and then haul me off. It's a saying that a peasant has a peasant's wit… Write down, too, your honour, that he hit me twice – in the jaw and in the chest.'

'When your hut was searched they found another nut… At what spot did you unscrew that, and when?'

'You mean the nut which lay under the red box?'

'I don't know where it was lying, only it was found. When did you unscrew it?'

'I didn't unscrew it; Ignashka, the son of one-eyed Semyon, gave it me. I mean the one which was under the box, but the one which was in the sledge in the yard Mitrofan and I unscrewed together.'

'What Mitrofan?'

'Mitrofan Petrov... Haven't you heard of him? He makes nets in our village and sells them to the gentry. He needs a lot of those nuts. Reckon a matter of ten for each net.'

'Listen. Article 1081 of the Penal Code lays down that every wilful damage of the railway line committed when it can expose the traffic on that line to danger, and the guilty party knows that an accident must be caused by it... (Do you understand? Knows! And you could not help knowing what this unscrewing would lead to...) is liable to penal servitude.'

'Of course, you know best... We are ignorant people... What do we understand?'

'You understand all about it! You are lying, shamming!'

'What should I lie for? Ask in the village if you don't believe me. Only a bleak is caught without a weight, and there is no fish worse than a gudgeon, yet even that won't bite without a weight.'

'You'd better tell me about the shillisper next,' said the magistrate, smiling.

'There are no shillispers in our parts... We cast our line without a weight on the top of the water with a butterfly; a mullet may be caught that way, though that is not often.'

'Come, hold your tongue.'

A silence follows. Denis shifts from one foot to the other, looks at the table with the green cloth on it, and blinks his eyes violently as though what was before him was not the cloth but the sun. The magistrate writes rapidly.

'Can I go?' asks Denis after a long silence.

'No. I must take you under guard and send you to prison.'

Denis leaves off blinking and, raising his thick eyebrows, looks inquiringly at the magistrate.

'How do you mean, to prison? Your honour! I have no time to spare, I must go to the fair; I must get three roubles from Yegor for some tallow!... '

'Hold your tongue; don't interrupt.'

'To prison... If there was something to go for, I'd go; but just to go for nothing! What for? I haven't stolen anything, I believe, and I've not been fighting… If you are in doubt about the arrears, your honour, don't believe the elder… You ask the agent… he's a regular heathen, the elder, you know.'

'Hold your tongue.'

I am holding my tongue, as it is,' mutters Denis; 'but that the elder has lied over the account, I'll take my oath for it… There are three of us brothers: Kuzma Grigoryev, then Yegor Grigoryev, and me, Denis Grigoryev.'

'You are hindering me… Hey, Semyon,' cries the magistrate, 'take him away!'

'There are three of us brothers,' mutters Denis, as two stalwart soldiers take him and lead him out of the room. 'A brother is not responsible for a brother. Kuzma does not pay, so you, Denis, must answer for it… Judges indeed! Our master the general is dead – the Kingdom of Heaven be his – or he would have shown you judges… You ought to judge sensibly, not at random… Flog if you like, but flog someone who deserves it, flog with conscience.'

The Cook's Wedding

Grisha, a fat, solemn little person of seven, was standing by the kitchen door listening and peeping through the keyhole. In the kitchen something extraordinary, and in his opinion never seen before, was taking place. A big, thick-set, red-haired peasant, with a beard, and a drop of perspiration on his nose, wearing a cabman's full coat, was sitting at the kitchen table on which they chopped the meat and sliced the onions. He was balancing a saucer on the five fingers of his right hand and drinking tea out of it, and crunching sugar so loudly that it sent a shiver down Grisha's back. Aksinya Stepanovna, the old nurse, was sitting on the dirty stool facing him, and she, too, was drinking tea. Her face was grave, though at the same time it beamed with a kind of triumph. Pelageya, the cook, was busy at the stove, and was apparently trying to hide her face. And on her face Grisha saw a regular illumination: it was burning and shifting through every shade of colour, beginning with a crimson purple and ending with a deathly white. She was continually catching hold of knives, forks, bits of wood, and rags with trembling hands, moving, grumbling to herself, making a clatter, but in reality doing nothing. She did not once glance at the table at which they were drinking tea, and to the questions put to her by the nurse she gave jerky, sullen answers without turning her face.

'Help yourself, Danilo Semyonitch,' the nurse urged him hospitably. 'Why do you keep on with tea and nothing but tea? You should have a drop of vodka!'

And nurse put before the visitor a bottle of vodka and a wine-glass, while her face wore a very wily expression.

'I never touch it… No… ' said the cabman, declining. 'Don't press me, Aksinya Stepanovna.'

'What a man!… A cabman and not drink!… A bachelor can't get on without drinking. Help yourself!'

The cabman looked askance at the bottle, then at nurse's wily face, and his own face assumed an expression no less cunning, as much as to say, 'You won't catch me, you old witch!'

'I don't drink; please excuse me. Such a weakness does not do in our calling. A man who works at a trade may drink, for he sits at home, but we cabmen are always in view of the public. Aren't we? If one goes into a pothouse one finds one's horse gone; if one takes a drop too much it is worse still; before you know where you are you will fall asleep or slip off the box. That's where it is.'

'And how much do you make a day, Danilo Semyonitch?'

'That's according. One day you will have a fare for three roubles, and another day you will come back to the yard without a farthing. The days are very different. Nowadays our business is no good. There are lots and lots of cabmen as you know, hay is dear, and folks are paltry nowadays and always contriving to go by tram. And yet, thank God, I have nothing to complain of. I have plenty to eat and good clothes to wear, and… we could even provide well for another… ' (the cabman stole a glance at Pelageya) 'if it were to their liking…'

Grisha did not hear what was said further. His mamma came to the door and sent him to the nursery to learn his lessons.

'Go and learn your lesson. It's not your business to listen here!'

When Grisha reached the nursery, he put 'My Own Book' in front of him, but he did not get on with his reading. All that he had just seen and heard aroused a multitude of questions in his mind.

'The cook's going to be married,' he thought. 'Strange – I don't understand what people get married for. Mamma was married to papa, Cousin Verotchka to Pavel Andreyitch. But one might be married to papa and Pavel Andreyitch after all: they have gold watch-chains and nice suits, their boots are always polished; but to marry that dreadful cabman with a red nose and felt boots… Fi! And why is it nurse wants poor Pelageya to be married?'

When the visitor had gone out of the kitchen, Pelageya appeared and began clearing away. Her agitation still persisted. Her face was red and looked scared. She scarcely touched the floor with the broom, and swept every corner five times over. She lingered for a long time in the room where mamma was sitting. She was evidently oppressed by her isolation, and she was longing to express herself, to share her impressions with someone, to open her heart.

'He's gone,' she muttered, seeing that mamma would not begin the conversation.

'One can see he is a good man,' said mamma, not taking her eyes off her sewing. 'Sober and steady.'

'I declare I won't marry him, mistress!' Pelageya cried suddenly, flushing crimson. 'I declare I won't!'

'Don't be silly; you are not a child. It's a serious step; you must think it over thoroughly, it's no use talking nonsense. Do you like him?'

'What an idea, mistress!' cried Pelageya, abashed. 'They say such things that… my goodness…'

'She should say she doesn't like him!' thought Grisha.

'What an affected creature you are… Do you like him?'

'But he is old, mistress!'

'Think of something else,' nurse flew out at her from the next room. 'He has not reached his fortieth year; and what do you want a young man for? Handsome is as handsome does… Marry him and that's all about it!'

'I swear I won't,' squealed Pelageya.

'You are talking nonsense. What sort of rascal do you want? Anyone else would have bowed down to his feet, and you declare you won't marry him. You want to be always winking at the postmen and tutors. That tutor that used to come to Grishenka, mistress… she was never tired of making eyes at him. O-o, the shameless hussy!'

'Have you seen this Danilo before?' mamma asked Pelageya.

'How could I have seen him? I set eyes on him today for the first time. Aksinya picked him up and brought him along… the accursed devil… And where has he come from for my undoing!'

At dinner, when Pelageya was handing the dishes, everyone looked into her face and teased her about the cabman. She turned fearfully red, and went off into a forced giggle.

'It must be shameful to get married,' thought Grisha. 'Terribly shameful.'

All the dishes were too salt, and blood oozed from the half-raw chickens, and, to cap it all, plates and knives kept dropping out of Pelageya's hands during dinner, as though from a shelf that had given way; but no one said a word of blame to her, as they all understood the state of her feelings. Only once papa flicked his table-napkin angrily and said to mamma:

'What do you want to be getting them all married for? What business is it of yours? Let them get married of themselves if they want to.'

After dinner, neighbouring cooks and maidservants kept flitting into the kitchen, and there was the sound of whispering till late evening. How they had scented out the matchmaking, God knows. When Grisha woke in the night he heard his nurse and the cook whispering together in the nursery. Nurse was talking persuasively, while the cook alternately sobbed and giggled. When he fell asleep after this, Grisha dreamed of Pelageya being carried off by Tchernomor and a witch.

Next day there was a calm. The life of the kitchen went on its accustomed way as though the cabman did not exist. Only from time to time nurse put on her new shawl, assumed a solemn and austere air, and went off somewhere for an hour or two, obviously to conduct negotiations… Pelageya did not see the cabman, and when his name was mentioned she flushed up and cried:

'May he be thrice damned! As though I should be thinking of him! Tfoo!'

In the evening mamma went into the kitchen, while nurse and Pelageya were zealously mincing something, and said:

'You can marry him, of course – that's your business – but I must tell you, Pelageya, that he cannot live here… You know I don't like to have anyone sitting in the kitchen. Mind now, remember… And I can't let you sleep out.'

'Goodness knows! What an idea, mistress!' shrieked the cook. 'Why do you keep throwing him up at me? Plague take him! He's a regular curse, confound him!…'

Glancing one Sunday morning into the kitchen, Grisha was struck dumb with amazement. The kitchen was crammed full of people. Here were cooks from the whole courtyard, the porter, two policemen, a non-commissioned officer with good-conduct stripes, and the boy Filka… This Filka was generally hanging about the laundry playing with the dogs; now he was combed and washed, and was holding an ikon in a tinfoil setting. Pelageya was standing in the middle of the kitchen in a new cotton dress, with a flower on her head. Beside her stood the cabman. The happy pair were red in the face and perspiring and blinking with embarrassment.

'Well… I fancy it is time,' said the non-commissioned officer, after a prolonged silence.

Pelageya's face worked all over and she began blubbering…

The soldier took a big loaf from the table, stood beside nurse, and began blessing the couple. The cabman went up to the soldier, flopped down on his knees, and gave a smacking kiss on his hand. He did the same before nurse. Pelageya followed him mechanically, and she too bowed down to the ground. At last the outer door was opened, there was a whiff of white mist, and the whole party flocked noisily out of the kitchen into the yard.

'Poor thing, poor thing,' thought Grisha, hearing the sobs of the cook. 'Where have they taken her? Why don't papa and mamma protect her?'

After the wedding there was singing and concertina-playing in the laundry till late evening. Mamma was cross all the evening because nurse smelt of vodka, and owing to the wedding there was no one to heat the samovar. Pelageya had not come back by the time Grisha went to bed.

'The poor thing is crying somewhere in the dark!' he thought. 'While the cabman is saying to her "shut up!"'

Next morning the cook was in the kitchen again. The cabman came in for a minute. He thanked mamma, and glancing sternly at Pelageya, said:

'Will you look after her, madam? Be a father and a mother to her. And you, too, Aksinya Stepanovna, do not forsake her, see that everything is as it should be… without any nonsense… And also, madam, if you would kindly advance me five roubles of her wages. I have got to buy a new horse-collar.'

Again a problem for Grisha: Pelageya was living in freedom, doing as she liked, and not having to account to anyone for her actions, and all at once, for no sort of reason, a stranger turns up, who has somehow acquired rights over her conduct and her property! Grisha was distressed. He longed passionately, almost to tears, to comfort this victim, as he supposed, of man's injustice. Picking out the very biggest apple in the store-room he stole into the kitchen, slipped it into Pelageya's hand, and darted headlong away.

Oh! The Public

'Here goes, I've done with drinking! Nothing… n-o-thing shall tempt me to it. It's time to take myself in hand; I must buck up and work… You're glad to get your salary, so you must do your work honestly, heartily, conscientiously, regardless of sleep and comfort. Chuck taking it easy. You've got into the way of taking a salary for nothing, my boy – that's not the right thing… not the right thing at all…'

After administering to himself several such lectures Podtyagin, the head ticket collector, begins to feel an irresistible impulse to get to work. It is past one o'clock at night, but in spite of that he wakes the ticket collectors and with them goes up and down the railway carriages, inspecting the tickets.

'T-t-t-ickets… P-p-p-please!' he keeps shouting, briskly snapping the clippers.

Sleepy figures, shrouded in the twilight of the railway carriages, start, shake their heads, and produce their tickets.

'T-t-t-tickets, please!' Podtyagin addresses a second-class passenger, a lean, scraggy-looking man, wrapped up in a fur coat and a rug and surrounded with pillows. 'Tickets, please!'

The scraggy-looking man makes no reply. He is buried in sleep. The head ticket-collector touches him on the shoulder and repeats impatiently: 'T-t-tickets, p-p-please!'

The passenger starts, opens his eyes, and gazes in alarm at Podtyagin.

'What?… Who?… Eh?'

'You're asked in plain language: t-t-tickets, p-p-please! If you please!'

'My God!' moans the scraggy-looking man, pulling a woebegone face. 'Good Heavens! I'm suffering from rheumatism… I haven't slept for three nights! I've just taken morphia on purpose to get to sleep, and you… with your tickets! It's merciless, it's inhuman! If you knew how hard it is for me to sleep you wouldn't disturb me for such nonsense… It's cruel, it's absurd! And what do you want with my ticket! It's positively stupid!'

Podtyagin considers whether to take offence or not – and decides to take offence.

'Don't shout here! This is not a tavern!'

'No, in a tavern people are more humane…' coughs the passenger. 'Perhaps you'll let me go to sleep another time! It's extraordinary: I've travelled abroad, all over the place, and no one asked for my ticket there, but here you're at it again and again, as though the devil were after you…'

'Well, you'd better go abroad again since you like it so much.'

'It's stupid, sir! Yes! As though it's not enough killing the passengers with fumes and stuffiness and draughts, they want to strangle us with red tape, too, damn it all! He must have the ticket! My goodness, what zeal! If it were of any use to the company – but half the passengers are travelling without a ticket!'

'Listen, sir!' cries Podtyagin, flaring up. 'If you don't leave off shouting and disturbing the public, I shall be obliged to put you out at the next station and to draw up a report on the incident!'

'This is revolting!' exclaims 'the public', growing indignant. 'Persecuting an invalid! Listen, and have some consideration!'

'But the gentleman himself was abusive!' says Podtyagin, a little scared. 'Very well… I won't take the ticket… as you like… Only, of course, as you know very well, it's my duty to do so… If it were not my duty, then, of course… You can ask the station-master… ask anyone you like…'

Podtyagin shrugs his shoulders and walks away from the invalid. At first he feels aggrieved and somewhat injured, then, after passing through two or three carriages, he begins to feel a certain uneasiness not unlike the pricking of conscience in his ticket-collector's bosom.

'There certainly was no need to wake the invalid,' he thinks, 'though it was not my fault… They imagine I did it wantonly, idly. They don't know that I'm bound in duty… if they don't believe it, I can bring the station-master to them.' A station. The train stops five minutes. Before the third bell, Podtyagin enters the same second-class carriage. Behind him stalks the station-master in a red cap.

'This gentleman here,' Podtyagin begins, 'declares that I have no right to ask for his ticket and… and is offended at it. I ask you, Mr. Station-master, to explain to him… Do I ask for tickets according to regulation or to please myself? Sir,' Podtyagin addresses the scraggy-looking man, 'sir! you can ask the station-master here if you don't believe me.'

The invalid starts as though he had been stung, opens his eyes, and with a woebegone face sinks back in his seat.

'My God! I have taken another powder and only just dozed off when here he is again… again! I beseech you have some pity on me!'

'You can ask the station-master… whether I have the right to demand your ticket or not.'

'This is insufferable! Take your ticket… take it! I'll pay for five extra if you'll only let me die in peace! Have you never been ill your-self? Heartless people!'

'This is simply persecution!' A gentleman in military uniform grows indignant. 'I can see no other explanation of this persistence.'

'Drop it…' says the station-master, frowning and pulling Podtyagin by the sleeve.

Podtyagin shrugs his shoulders and slowly walks after the station-master.

'There's no pleasing them!' he thinks, bewildered. 'It was for his sake I brought the station-master, that he might understand and be pacified, and he… swears!'

Another station. The train stops ten minutes. Before the second bell, while Podtyagin is standing at the refreshment bar, drinking seltzer water, two gentlemen go up to him, one in the uniform of an engineer, and the other in a military overcoat.

'Look here, ticket-collector!' the engineer begins, addressing Podtyagin. 'Your behaviour to that invalid passenger has revolted all who witnessed it. My name is Puzitsky; I am an engineer, and this gentleman is a colonel. If you do not apologise to the passenger, we shall make a complaint to the traffic manager, who is a friend of ours.'

'Gentlemen! Why of course I... why of course you... ' Podtyagin is panic-stricken.

'We don't want explanations. But we warn you, if you don't apologise, we shall see justice done to him.'

Certainly I... I'll apologise, of course... To be sure...'

Half an hour later, Podtyagin having thought of an apologetic phrase which would satisfy the passenger without lowering his own dignity, walks into the carriage. 'Sir,' he addresses the invalid. 'Listen, sir...'

The invalid starts and leaps up: 'What?'

'I... what was it?... You mustn't be offended...'

'Och! Water... ' gasps the invalid, clutching at his heart. 'I'd just taken a third dose of morphia, dropped asleep, and... again! Good God! when will this torture cease!'

'I only... you must excuse... '

'Oh!... Put me out at the next station! I can't stand any more... I... I am dying...'

'This is mean, disgusting!' cry the 'public,' revolted. 'Go away! You shall pay for such persecution. Get away!'

Podtyagin waves his hand in despair, sighs, and walks out of the carriage. He goes to the attendants' compartment, sits down at the table, exhausted, and complains:

'Oh, the public! There's no satisfying them! It's no use working and doing one's best! One's driven to drinking and cursing it all... If you do nothing – they're angry; if you begin doing your duty, they're angry too. There's nothing for it but drink!'

Podtyagin empties a bottle straight off and thinks no more of work, duty, and honesty!

Children

Papa and mamma and Aunt Nadya are not at home. They have gone to a christening party at the house of that old officer who rides on a little grey horse. While waiting for them to come home, Grisha, Anya, Alyosha, Sonya, and the cook's son, Andrey, are sitting at the table in the dining-room, playing at lotto. To tell the truth, it is bedtime, but how can one go to sleep without hearing from mamma what the baby was like at the christening, and what they had for supper? The table, lighted by a hanging lamp, is dotted with numbers, nutshells, scraps of paper, and little bits of glass. Two cards lie in front of each player, and a heap of bits of glass for covering the numbers. In the middle of the table is a white saucer with five kopecks in it. Beside the saucer, a half-eaten apple, a pair of scissors, and a plate on which they have been told to put their nutshells. The children are playing for money. The stake is a kopeck. The rule is: if anyone cheats, he is turned out at once. There is no one in the dining-room but the players, and nurse, Agafya Ivanovna, is in the kitchen, showing the cook how to cut a pattern, while their elder brother, Vasya, a schoolboy in the fifth class, is lying on the sofa in the drawing-room, feeling bored.

They are playing with zest. The greatest excitement is expressed on the face of Grisha. He is a small boy of nine, with a head cropped so that the bare skin shows through, chubby cheeks, and thick lips like a negro's. He is already in the preparatory class, and so is regarded as grown up, and the cleverest. He is playing entirely for the sake of the money. If there had been no kopecks in the saucer, he would have been asleep long ago. His brown eyes stray uneasily and jealously over the other players' cards. The fear that he may not win, envy, and the financial combinations of which his cropped head is full, will not let him sit still and concentrate his mind. He fidgets as though he were sitting on thorns. When he wins, he snatches up the money greedily, and instantly puts it in his pocket. His sister, Anya, a girl of eight, with a sharp chin and clever shining eyes, is also afraid that someone else may win. She flushes and turns pale, and watches the players keenly. The kopecks do not interest her. Success in the game is for her a question of vanity. The other sister, Sonya, a child of six with a curly head, and a complexion such as is seen only in very healthy children, expensive dolls, and the faces on bonbon boxes, is playing lotto for the process of the game itself. There is bliss all over her face. Whoever wins, she laughs and claps her hands. Alyosha, a chubby, spherical little figure, gasps, breathes hard through his nose, and stares open-eyed at the cards. He is moved neither by covetousness nor vanity. So long as he is not driven out of the room, or sent to bed, he is thankful. He looks phlegmatic, but at heart he is rather a little beast. He is not there so much for the sake of the lotto, as for the sake of the misunder-standings which are inevitable in the game. He is greatly delighted if one hits another, or calls him names. He ought to have run off some-where long ago, but he won't leave the table for a minute, for fear they should steal his counters or his kopecks. As he can only count the units and numbers which end in nought, Anya covers his numbers for him. The fifth player, the cook's son, Andrey, a dark-skinned and sickly looking boy in a cotton shirt, with a copper cross on his breast, stands motionless, looking dreamily at the numbers. He takes no interest in winning, or in the success of the others, because he is entirely engrossed by the arithmetic of the game, and its far from complex theory; 'How many numbers there are in the world,' he is thinking, 'and how is it they don't get mixed up?'

They all shout out the numbers in turn, except Sonya and Alyosha. To vary the monotony, they have invented in the course of time a number of synonyms and comic nicknames. Seven, for instance, is called the 'ovenrake', eleven the 'sticks', seventy-seven 'Semyon Semyonitch', ninety 'grandfather', and so on. The game is going merrily.

'Thirty-two,' cries Grisha, drawing the little yellow cylinders out of his father's cap. 'Seventeen! Ovenrake! Twenty-eight! Lay them straight…'

Anya sees that Andrey has let twenty-eight slip. At any other time she would have pointed it out to him, but now when her vanity lies in the saucer with the kopecks, she is triumphant.

'Twenty-three!' Grisha goes on, 'Semyon Semyonitch! Nine!'

'A beetle, a beetle,' cries Sonya, pointing to a beetle running across the table. 'Aie!'

'Don't kill it,' says Alyosha, in his deep bass, 'perhaps it's got children…'

Sonya follows the black beetle with her eyes and wonders about its children: what tiny little beetles they must be!

'Forty-three! One!' Grisha goes on, unhappy at the thought that Anya has already made two fours. 'Six!'

'Game! I have got the game!' cries Sonya, rolling her eyes coquettishly and giggling.

The players' countenances lengthen.

'Must make sure!' says Grisha, looking with hatred at Sonya.

Exercising his rights as a big boy, and the cleverest, Grisha takes upon himself to decide. What he wants, that they do. Sonya's reckoning is slowly and carefully verified, and to the great regret of her fellow players, it appears that she has not cheated. Another game is begun.

'I did see something yesterday!' says Anya, as though to herself. 'Filipp Filippitch turned his eyelids inside out somehow and his eyes looked red and dreadful, like an evil spirit's.'

'I saw it too,' says Grisha. 'Eight! And a boy at our school can move his ears. Twenty-seven!'

Andrey looks up at Grisha, meditates, and says:

'I can move my ears too…'

'Well then, move them.'

Andrey moves his eyes, his lips, and his fingers, and fancies that his ears are moving too. Everyone laughs.

'He is a horrid man, that Filipp Filippitch,' sighs Sonya. 'He came into our nursery yesterday, and I had nothing on but my chemise … And I felt so improper!'

'Game!' Grisha cries suddenly, snatching the money from the saucer. 'I've got the game! You can look and see if you like.'

The cook's son looks up and turns pale.

'Then I can't go on playing any more,' he whispers.

'Why not?'

'Because… because I have got no more money.'

'You can't play without money,' says Grisha.

Andrey ransacks his pockets once more to make sure. Finding nothing in them but crumbs and a bitten pencil, he drops the corners of his mouth and begins blinking miserably. He is on the point of crying…

'I'll put it down for you!' says Sonya, unable to endure his look of agony. 'Only mind you must pay me back afterwards.'

The money is brought and the game goes on.

'I believe they are ringing somewhere,' says Anya, opening her eyes wide.

They all leave off playing and gaze open-mouthed at the dark window. The reflection of the lamp glimmers in the darkness.

'It was your fancy.'

'At night they only ring in the cemetery,' says Andrey.

'And what do they ring there for?'

'To prevent robbers from breaking into the church. They are afraid of the bells.'

'And what do robbers break into the church for?' asks Sonya.

'Everyone knows what for: to kill the watchmen.'

A minute passes in silence. They all look at one another, shudder, and go on playing. This time Andrey wins.

'He has cheated,' Alyosha booms out, apropos of nothing.

'What a lie, I haven't cheated.'

Andrey turns pale, his mouth works, and he gives Alyosha a slap on the head! Alyosha glares angrily, jumps up, and with one knee on the table, slaps Andrey on the cheek! Each gives the other a second blow, and both howl. Sonya, feeling such horrors too much for her, begins crying too, and the dining-room resounds with lamentations on various notes. But do not imagine that that is the end of the game. Before five minutes are over, the children are laughing and talking peaceably again. Their faces are tear-stained, but that does not prevent them from smiling; Alyosha is positively blissful, there has been a squabble!

Vasya, the fifth form schoolboy, walks into the dining-room. He looks sleepy and disillusioned.

'This is revolting!' he thinks, seeing Grisha feel in his pockets in which the kopecks are jingling. 'How can they give children money? And how can they let them play games of chance? A nice way to bring them up, I must say! It's revolting!'

But the children's play is so tempting that he feels an inclination to join them and to try his luck.

'Wait a minute and I'll sit down to a game,' he says.

'Put down a kopeck!'

'In a minute,' he says, fumbling in his pockets. 'I haven't a kopeck, but here is a rouble. I'll stake a rouble.'

'No, no, no… You must put down a kopeck.'

'You stupids. A rouble is worth more than a kopeck anyway,' the schoolboy explains. 'Whoever wins can give me change.'

'No, please! Go away!'

The fifth form schoolboy shrugs his shoulders, and goes into the kitchen to get change from the servants. It appears there is not a single kopeck in the kitchen.

'In that case, you give me change,' he urges Grisha, coming back from the kitchen. 'I'll pay you for the change. Won't you? Come, give me ten kopecks for a rouble.'

Grisha looks suspiciously at Vasya, wondering whether it isn't some trick, a swindle.

'I won't,' he says, holding his pockets.

Vasya begins to get cross, and abuses them, calling them idiots and blockheads.

'I'll put down a stake for you, Vasya! ' says Sonya. 'Sit down.' He sits down and lays two cards before him. Anya begins counting the numbers.

'I've dropped a kopeck!' Grisha announces suddenly, in an agitated voice. 'Wait!'

He takes the lamp, and creeps under the table to look for the kopeck. They clutch at nutshells and all sorts of nastiness, knock their heads together, but do not find the kopeck. They begin looking again, and look till Vasya takes the lamp out of Grisha's hands and puts it in its place. Grisha goes on looking in the dark. But at last the kopeck is found. The players sit down at the table and mean to go on playing.

'Sonya is asleep!' Alyosha announces.

Sonya, with her curly head lying on her arms, is in a sweet, sound, tranquil sleep, as though she had been asleep for an hour. She has fallen asleep by accident, while the others were looking for the kopeck.

'Come along, lie on mamma's bed!' says Anya, leading her away from the table. 'Come along!'

They all troop out with her, and five minutes later mamma's bed presents a curious spectacle. Sonya is asleep. Alyosha is snoring beside her. With their heads to the others' feet, sleep Grisha and Anya. The cook's son, Andrey too, has managed to snuggle in beside them. Near them lie the kopecks, that have lost their power till the next game. Goodnight!

Misery

'*To whom shall I tell my grief?*'

The twilight of evening. Big flakes of wet snow are whirling lazily about the street lamps, which have just been lighted, and lying in a thin soft layer on roofs, horses' backs, shoulders, caps. Iona Potapov, the sledge-driver, is all white like a ghost. He sits on the box without stirring, bent as double as the living body can be bent. If a regular snowdrift fell on him it seems as though even then he would not think it necessary to shake it off… His little mare is white and motionless too. Her stillness, the angularity of her lines, and the stick-like straightness of her legs make her look like a halfpenny gingerbread horse. She is probably lost in thought. Anyone who has been torn away from the plough, from the familiar gray landscapes, and cast into this slough, full of monstrous lights, of unceasing uproar and hurrying people, is bound to think.

It is a long time since Iona and his nag have budged. They came out of the yard before dinnertime and not a single fare yet. But now the shades of evening are falling on the town. The pale light of the street lamps changes to a vivid color, and the bustle of the street grows noisier.

'Sledge to Vyborgskaya!' Iona hears. 'Sledge!'

Iona starts, and through his snow-plastered eyelashes sees an officer in a military overcoat with a hood over his head.

'To Vyborgskaya,' repeats the officer. 'Are you asleep? To Vyborgskaya!'

In token of assent Iona gives a tug at the reins which sends cakes of snow flying from the horse's back and shoulders. The officer gets into the sledge. The sledge-driver clicks to the horse, cranes his neck like a swan, rises in his seat, and more from habit than necessity brandishes his whip. The mare cranes her neck, too, crooks her stick-like legs, and hesitatingly sets of…

'Where are you shoving, you devil?' Iona immediately hears shouts from the dark mass shifting to and fro before him. 'Where the devil are you going? Keep to the r-right!'

'You don't know how to drive! Keep to the right,' says the officer angrily.

A coachman driving a carriage swears at him; a pedestrian crossing the road and brushing the horse's nose with his shoulder looks at him angrily and shakes the snow off his sleeve. Iona fidgets on the box as though he were sitting on thorns, jerks his elbows, and turns his eyes about like one possessed as though he did not know where he was or why he was there.

'What rascals they all are!' says the officer jocosely. 'They are simply doing their best to run up against you or fall under the horse's feet. They must be doing it on purpose.'

Iona looks as his fare and moves his lips… Apparently he means to say something, but nothing comes but a sniff.

'What?' inquires the officer.

Iona gives a wry smile, and straining his throat, brings out huskily: 'My son… er… my son died this week, sir.'

'H'm! What did he die of?'

Iona turns his whole body round to his fare, and says:

'Who can tell! It must have been from fever… He lay three days in the hospital and then he died… God's will.'

'Turn round, you devil!' comes out of the darkness. 'Have you gone cracked, you old dog? Look where you are going!'

'Drive on! drive on!…' says the officer. 'We shan't get there till tomorrow going on like this. Hurry up!'

The sledge-driver cranes his neck again, rises in his seat, and with heavy grace swings his whip. Several times he looks round at the officer, but the latter keeps his eyes shut and is apparently disinclined to listen. Putting his fare down at Vyborgskaya, Iona stops by a restaurant, and again sits huddled up on the box… Again the wet snow paints him and his horse white. One hour passes, and then another…

Three young men, two tall and thin, one short and hunchbacked, come up, railing at each other and loudly stamping on the pavement with their goloshes.

'Cabby, to the Police Bridge!' the hunchback cries in a cracked voice. 'The three of us,… twenty kopecks!'

Iona tugs at the reins and clicks to his horse. Twenty kopecks is not a fair price, but he has no thoughts for that. Whether it is a rouble or whether it is five kopecks does not matter to him now so long as he has a fare… The three young men, shoving each other and using bad language, go up to the sledge, and all three try to sit down at once. The question remains to be settled: Which are to sit down and which one is to stand? After a long altercation, ill-temper, and abuse, they come to the conclusion that the hunchback must stand because he is the shortest.

'Well, drive on,' says the hunchback in his cracked voice, settling himself and breathing down Iona's neck. 'Cut along! What a cap you've got, my friend! You wouldn't find a worse one in all Petersburg…'

'He-he!… he-he!… ' laughs Iona. 'It's nothing to boast of!'

'Well, then, nothing to boast of, drive on! Are you going to drive like this all the way? Eh? Shall I give you one in the neck?'

'My head aches,' says one of the tall ones. 'At the Dukmasovs' yesterday Vaska and I drank four bottles of brandy between us.'

'I can't make out why you talk such stuff,' says the other tall one angrily. 'You lie like a brute.'

'Strike me dead, it's the truth!… '

'It's about as true as that a louse coughs.'

'He-he!' grins Iona. 'Me-er-ry gentlemen!'

'Tfoo! the devil take you!' cries the hunchback indignantly. 'Will you get on, you old plague, or won't you? Is that the way to drive? Give her one with the whip. Hang it all, give it her well.'

Iona feels behind his back the jolting person and quivering voice of the hunchback. He hears abuse addressed to him, he sees people, and the feeling of loneliness begins little by little to be less heavy on his heart. The hunchback swears at him, till he chokes over some elaborately whimsical string of epithets and is overpowered by his cough. His tall companions begin talking of a certain Nadyezhda Petrovna. Iona looks round at them. Waiting till there is a brief pause, he looks round once more and says:

'This week... er... my... er... son died!'

'We shall all die,...' says the hunchback with a sigh, wiping his lips after coughing. 'Come, drive on! drive on! My friends, I simply cannot stand crawling like this! When will he get us there?'

'Well, you give him a little encouragement... one in the neck!'

'Do you hear, you old plague? I'll make you smart. If one stands on ceremony with fellows like you one may as well walk. Do you hear, you old dragon? Or don't you care a hang what we say? '

And Iona hears rather than feels a slap on the back of his neck.

'He-he!...' he laughs. 'Merry gentlemen... God give you health!'

'Cabman, are you married?' asks one of the tall ones.

'I? He he! Me-er-ry gentlemen. The only wife for me now is the damp earth... He-ho-ho!...The grave that is!... Here my son's dead and I am alive... It's a strange thing, death has come in at the wrong door... Instead of coming for me it went for my son...'

And Iona turns round to tell them how his son died, but at that point the hunchback gives a faint sigh and announces that, thank God! they have arrived at last. After taking his twenty kopecks, Iona gazes for a long while after the revelers, who disappear into a dark entry. Again he is alone and again there is silence for him... The misery which has been for a brief space eased comes back again and tears his heart more cruelly than ever. With a look of anxiety and suffering Iona's eyes stray restlessly among the crowds moving to and fro on both sides of the street: can he not find among those thousands someone who will listen to him? But the crowds flit by heedless of him and his misery… His misery is immense, beyond all bounds. If Iona's heart were to burst and his misery to flow out, it would flood the whole world, it seems, but yet it is not seen. It has found a hiding-place in such an insignificant shell that one would not have found it with a candle by daylight…

Iona sees a house-porter with a parcel and makes up his mind to address him.

'What time will it be, friend?' he asks.

'Going on for ten… Why have you stopped here? Drive on!'

Iona drives a few paces away, bends himself double, and gives himself up to his misery. He feels it is no good to appeal to people. But before five minutes have passed he draws himself up, shakes his head as though he feels a sharp pain, and tugs at the reins… He can bear it no longer.

'Back to the yard!' he thinks. 'To the yard!'

And his little mare, as though she knew his thoughts, falls to trotting. An hour and a half later Iona is sitting by a big dirty stove. On the stove, on the floor, and on the benches are people snoring. The air is full of smells and stuffiness. Iona looks at the sleeping figures, scratches himself, and regrets that he has come home so early…

'I have not earned enough to pay for the oats, even,' he thinks. 'That's why I am so miserable. A man who knows how to do his work, …who has had enough to eat, and whose horse has had enough to eat, is always at ease…'

In one of the corners a young cabman gets up, clears his throat sleepily, and makes for the water-bucket.

'Want a drink?' Iona asks him.

'Seems so.'

'May it do you good… But my son is dead, mate… Do you hear? This week in the hospital… It's a queer business…'

Iona looks to see the effect produced by his words, but he sees nothing. The young man has covered his head over and is already asleep. The old man sighs and scratches himself… Just as the young man had been thirsty for water, he thirsts for speech. His son will soon have been dead a week, and he has not really talked to anybody yet

... He wants to talk of it properly, with deliberation... He wants to tell how his son was taken ill, how he suffered, what he said before he died, how he died... He wants to describe the funeral, and how he went to the hospital to get his son's clothes. He still has his daughter Anisya in the country... And he wants to talk about her too... Yes, he has plenty to talk about now. His listener ought to sigh and exclaim and lament... It would be even better to talk to women. Though they are silly creatures, they blubber at the first word.

'Let's go out and have a look at the mare,' Iona thinks. 'There is always time for sleep... You'll have sleep enough, no fear...'

He puts on his coat and goes into the stables where his mare is standing. He thinks about oats, about hay, about the weather... He cannot think about his son when he is alone... To talk about him with someone is possible, but to think of him and picture him is insufferable anguish...

'Are you munching?' Iona asks his mare, seeing her shining eyes. 'There, munch away, munch away... Since we have not earned enough for oats, we will eat hay... Yes, ...I have grown too old to drive... My son ought to be driving, not I... He was a real cabman... He ought to have lived...'

Iona is silent for a while, and then he goes on:

'That's how it is, old girl... Kuzma Ionitch is gone... He said goodbye to me... He went and died for no reason... Now, suppose you had a little colt, and you were own mother to that little colt... And all at once that same little colt went and died... You'd be sorry, wouldn't you? . . .'

The little mare munches, listens, and breathes on her master's hands. Iona is carried away and tells her all about it.

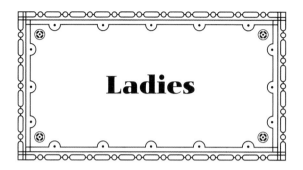

Ladies

Fyodor Petrovitch the Director of Elementary Schools in the N. District, who considered himself a just and generous man, was one day interviewing in his office a schoolmaster called Vremensky.

'No, Mr. Vremensky,' he was saying, 'your retirement is inevitable. You cannot continue your work as a schoolmaster with a voice like that! How did you come to lose it?'

'I drank cold beer when I was in a perspiration…' hissed the schoolmaster.

'What a pity! After a man has served fourteen years, such a calamity all at once! The idea of a career being ruined by such a trivial thing. What are you intending to do now?'

The schoolmaster made no answer.

'Are you a family man?' asked the director.

'A wife and two children, your Excellency…' hissed the schoolmaster.

A silence followed. The director got up from the table and walked to and fro in perturbation.

'I cannot think what I am going to do with you!' he said. 'A teacher you cannot be, and you are not yet entitled to a pension… To abandon you to your fate, and leave you to do the best you can, is rather awkward. We look on you as one of our men, you have served fourteen years, so it is our business to help you… But how are we to help you? What can I do for you? Put yourself in my place: what can I do for you?'

A silence followed; the director walked up and down, still thinking, and Vremensky, overwhelmed by his trouble, sat on the edge of his chair, and he, too, thought. All at once the director began beaming, and even snapped his fingers.

'I wonder I did not think of it before!' he began rapidly. 'Listen, this is what I can offer you. Next week our secretary at the Home is retiring. If you like, you can have his place! There you are!'

Vremensky, not expecting such good fortune, beamed too.

'That's capital,' said the director. 'Write the application today.'

Dismissing Vremensky, Fyodor Petrovitch felt relieved and even gratified: the bent figure of the hissing schoolmaster was no longer confronting him, and it was agreeable to recognize that in offering a vacant post to Vremensky he had acted fairly and conscientiously, like a good-hearted and thoroughly decent person. But this agreeable state of mind did not last long. When he went home and sat down to dinner his wife, Nastasya Ivanovna, said suddenly:

'Oh yes, I was almost forgetting! Nina Sergeyevna came to see me yesterday and begged for your interest on behalf of a young man. I am told there is a vacancy in our Home…'

Yes, but the post has already been promised to someone else,' said the director, and he frowned. 'And you know my rule: I never give posts through patronage.'

'I know, but for Nina Sergeyevna, I imagine, you might make an exception. She loves us as though we were relations, and we have never done anything for her. And don't think of refusing, Fedya! You will wound both her and me with your whims.'

'Who is it that she is recommending?'

'Polzuhin!'

'What Polzuhin? Is it that fellow who played Tchatsky at the party on New Year's Day? Is it that gentleman? Not on any account!'

The director left off eating.

'Not on any account!' he repeated. 'Heaven preserve us!'

'But why not?'

'Understand, my dear, that if a young man does not set to work directly, but through women, he must be good for nothing! Why doesn't he come to me himself?'

After dinner the director lay on the sofa in his study and began reading the letters and newspapers he had received.

'Dear Fyodor Petrovitch,' wrote the wife of the Mayor of the town. 'You once said that I knew the human heart and understood people. Now you have an opportunity of verifying this in practice. K. N. Polzuhin, whom I know to be an excellent young man, will call upon you in a day or two to ask you for the post of secretary at our Home. He is a very nice youth. If you take an interest in him you will be convinced of it.' And so on.

'On no account!' was the director's comment. 'Heaven preserve me!'

After that, not a day passed without the director's receiving letters recommending Polzuhin. One fine morning Polzuhin himself, a stout young man with a close-shaven face like a jockey's, in a new black suit, made his appearance…

'I see people on business not here but at the office,' said the director drily, on hearing his request.

'Forgive me, your Excellency, but our common acquaintances advised me to come here.'

'H'm!' growled the director, looking with hatred at the pointed toes of the young man's shoes. 'To the best of my belief your father is a man of property and you are not in want,' he said. 'What induces you to ask for this post? The salary is very trifling!'

'It's not for the sake of the salary… It's a government post, any way…'

'H'm… It strikes me that within a month you will be sick of the job and you will give it up, and meanwhile there are candidates for whom it would be a career for life. There are poor men for whom…'

'I shan't get sick of it, your Excellency,' Polzuhin interposed. 'Honour bright, I will do my best!'

It was too much for the director.

'Tell me,' he said, smiling contemptuously, 'why was it you didn't apply to me direct but thought fitting instead to trouble ladies as a preliminary?'

'I didn't know that it would be disagreeable to you,' Polzuhin answered, and he was embarrassed. 'But, your Excellency, if you attach no significance to letters of recommendation, I can give you a testimonial...'

He drew from his pocket a letter and handed it to the director. At the bottom of the testimonial, which was written in official language and handwriting, stood the signature of the Governor. Everything pointed to the Governor's having signed it unread, simply to get rid of some importunate lady.

'There's nothing for it, I bow to his authority...I obey...' said the director, reading the testimonial, and he heaved a sigh.

'Send in your application tomorrow... There's nothing to be done...'

And when Polzuhin had gone out, the director abandoned himself to a feeling of repulsion.

'Sneak!' he hissed, pacing from one corner to the other. 'He has got what he wanted, one way or the other, the good-for-nothing toady! Making up to the ladies! Reptile! Creature!'

The director spat loudly in the direction of the door by which Polzuhin had departed, and was immediately overcome with embarrassment, for at that moment a lady, the wife of the Superintendent of the Provincial Treasury, walked in at the door.

'I've come for a tiny minute ...a tiny minute...' began the lady. 'Sit down, friend, and listen to me attentively... Well, I've been told you have a post vacant... Today or tomorrow you will receive a visit from a young man called Polzuhin...'

The lady chattered on, while the director gazed at her with lustreless, stupefied eyes like a man on the point of fainting, gazed and smiled from politeness.

And the next day when Vremensky came to his office it was a long time before the director could bring himself to tell the truth. He hesitated, was incoherent, and could not think how to begin or what to say. He wanted to apologize to the schoolmaster, to tell him the whole truth, but his tongue halted like a drunkard's, his ears burned, and he was suddenly overwhelmed with vexation and resentment that he should have to play such an absurd part – in his own office, before his subordinate. He suddenly brought his fist down on the table, leaped up, and shouted angrily:

'I have no post for you! I have not, and that's all about it! Leave me in peace! Don't worry me! Be so good as to leave me alone!'

And he walked out of the office.

The Chorus Girl

One day when she was younger and better-looking, and when her voice was stronger, Nikolay Petrovitch Kolpakov, her adorer, was sitting in the outer room in her summer villa. It was intolerably hot and stifling. Kolpakov, who had just dined and drunk a whole bottle of inferior port, felt ill-humoured and out of sorts. Both were bored and waiting for the heat of the day to be over in order to go for a walk.

All at once there was a sudden ring at the door. Kolpakov, who was sitting with his coat off, in his slippers, jumped up and looked inquiringly at Pasha.

'It must be the postman or one of the girls,' said the singer.

Kolpakov did not mind being found by the postman or Pasha's lady friends, but by way of precaution gathered up his clothes and went into the next room, while Pasha ran to open the door. To her great surprise in the doorway stood, not the postman and not a girl friend, but an unknown woman, young and beautiful, who was dressed like a lady, and from all outward signs was one.

The stranger was pale and was breathing heavily as though she had been running up a steep flight of stairs.

'What is it?' asked Pasha.

The lady did not at once answer. She took a step forward, slowly looked about the room, and sat down in a way that suggested that from fatigue, or perhaps illness, she could not stand; then for a long time her pale lips quivered as she tried in vain to speak.

'Is my husband here?' she asked at last, raising to Pasha her big eyes with their red tear-stained lids.

'Husband?' whispered Pasha, and was suddenly so frightened that her hands and feet turned cold. 'What husband?' she repeated, beginning to tremble.

'My husband... Nikolay Petrovitch Kolpakov.'

'N... no, madam... I... I don't know any husband.'

A minute passed in silence. The stranger several times passed her handkerchief over her pale lips and held her breath to stop her inward trembling, while Pasha stood before her motionless, like a post, and looked at her with astonishment and terror.

'So you say he is not here?' the lady asked, this time speaking with a firm voice and smiling oddly.

'I... I don't know who it is you are asking about.'

'You are horrid, mean, vile... ' the stranger muttered, scanning Pasha with hatred and repulsion. 'Yes, yes... you are horrid. I am very, very glad that at last I can tell you so!'

Pasha felt that on this lady in black with the angry eyes and white slender fingers she produced the impression of something horrid and unseemly, and she felt ashamed of her chubby red cheeks, the pockmark on her nose, and the fringe on her forehead, which never could be combed back. And it seemed to her that if she had been thin, and had had no powder on her face and no fringe on her forehead, then she could have disguised the fact that she was not 'respectable,' and she would not have felt so frightened and ashamed to stand facing this unknown, mysterious lady.

'Where is my husband?' the lady went on. 'Though I don't care whether he is here or not, but I ought to tell you that the money has been missed, and they are looking for Nikolay Petrovitch… They mean to arrest him. That's your doing!'

The lady got up and walked about the room in great excitement. Pasha looked at her and was so frightened that she could not understand.

'He'll be found and arrested today,' said the lady, and she gave a sob, and in that sound could be heard her resentment and vexation. 'I know who has brought him to this awful position! Low, horrid creature! Loathsome, mercenary hussy!' The lady's lips worked and her nose wrinkled up with disgust. 'I am helpless, do you hear, you low woman?… I am helpless; you are stronger than I am, but there is One to defend me and my children! God sees all! He is just! He will punish you for every tear I have shed, for all my sleepless nights! The time will come; you will think of me!…'

Silence followed again. The lady walked about the room and wrung her hands, while Pasha still gazed blankly at her in amazement, not understanding and expecting something terrible.

'I know nothing about it, madam,' she said, and suddenly burst into tears.

'You are lying!' cried the lady, and her eyes flashed angrily at her. 'I know all about it! I've known you a long time. I know that for the last month he has been spending every day with you!'

'Yes. What then? What of it? I have a great many visitors, but I don't force anyone to come. He is free to do as he likes.'

'I tell you they have discovered that money is missing! He has embezzled money at the office! For the sake of such a… creature as you, for your sake he has actually committed a crime. Listen,' said the lady in a resolute voice, stopping short, facing Pasha. 'You can have no principles; you live simply to do harm – that's your object; but one can't imagine you have fallen so low that you have no trace of human feeling left! He has a wife, children… If he is condemned and sent into exile we shall starve, the children and I… Understand that! And yet there is a chance of saving him and us from destitution and disgrace. If I take them nine hundred roubles today they will let him alone. Only nine hundred roubles!'

'What nine hundred roubles?' Pasha asked softly. 'I… I don't know… I haven't taken it.'

'I am not asking you for nine hundred roubles… You have no

money, and I don't want your money. I ask you for something else… Men usually give expensive things to women like you. Only give me back the things my husband has given you!'

'Madam, he has never made me a present of anything!' Pasha wailed, beginning to understand.

'Where is the money? He has squandered his own and mine and other people's… What has become of it all? Listen, I beg you! I was carried away by indignation and have said a lot of nasty things to you, but I apologise. You must hate me, I know, but if you are capable of sympathy, put yourself in my position! I implore you to give me back the things!'

'H'm!' said Pasha, and she shrugged her shoulders. 'I would with pleasure, but God is my witness, he never made me a present of anything. Believe me, on my conscience. However, you are right, though,' said the singer in confusion, 'he did bring me two little things. Certainly I will give them back, if you wish it.'

Pasha pulled out one of the drawers in the toilet-table and took out of it a hollow gold bracelet and a thin ring with a ruby in it.

'Here, madam!' she said, handing the visitor these articles.

The lady flushed and her face quivered. She was offended.

'What are you giving me?' she said. 'I am not asking for charity, but for what does not belong to you… what you have taken advantage of your position to squeeze out of my husband… that weak, unhappy man… On Thursday, when I saw you with my husband at the harbour you were wearing expensive brooches and bracelets. So it's no use your playing the innocent lamb to me! I ask you for the last time: will you give me the things, or not?'

'You are a queer one, upon my word,' said Pasha, beginning to feel offended. 'I assure you that, except the bracelet and this little ring, I've never seen a thing from your Nikolay Petrovitch. He brings me nothing but sweet cakes.'

'Sweet cakes!' laughed the stranger. 'At home the children have nothing to eat, and here you have sweet cakes. You absolutely refuse to restore the presents?'

Receiving no answer, the lady sat, down and stared into space, pondering.

'What's to be done now?' she said. 'If I don't get nine hundred roubles, he is ruined, and the children and I am ruined, too. Shall I kill this low woman or go down on my knees to her?'

The lady pressed her handkerchief to her face and broke into sobs.

'I beg you!' Pasha heard through the stranger's sobs. 'You see you have plundered and ruined my husband. Save him… You have no feeling for him, but the children… the children… What have the children done?'

Pasha imagined little children standing in the street, crying with hunger, and she, too, sobbed.

'What can I do, madam?' she said. 'You say that I am a low woman and that I have ruined Nikolay Petrovitch, and I assure you… before God Almighty, I have had nothing from him whatever… There is only one girl in our chorus who has a rich admirer; all the rest of us live from hand to mouth on bread and kvass. Nikolay Petrovitch is a highly educated, refined gentleman, so I've made him welcome. We are bound to make gentlemen welcome.'

'I ask you for the things! Give me the things! I am crying… I am humiliating myself… If you like I will go down on my knees! If you wish it!'

Pasha shrieked with horror and waved her hands. She felt that this pale, beautiful lady who expressed herself so grandly, as though she were on the stage, really might go down on her knees to her, simply from pride, from grandeur, to exalt herself and humiliate the chorus girl.

'Very well, I will give you things!' said Pasha, wiping her eyes and bustling about. 'By all means. Only they are not from Nikolay Petrovitch… I got these from other gentlemen. As you please…'

Pasha pulled out the upper drawer of the chest, took out a diamond brooch, a coral necklace, some rings and bracelets, and gave them all to the lady.

'Take them if you like, only I've never had anything from your husband. Take them and grow rich,' Pasha went on, offended at the threat to go down on her knees. 'And if you are a lady… his lawful wife, you should keep him to yourself. I should think so! I did not ask him to come; he came of himself.'

Through her tears the lady scrutinized the articles given her and said:

'This isn't everything… There won't be five hundred roubles' worth here.'

Pasha impulsively flung out of the chest a gold watch, a cigar-case and studs, and said, flinging up her hands:

'I've nothing else left… You can search!'

The visitor gave a sigh, with trembling hands twisted the things up in her handkerchief, and went out without uttering a word, without even nodding her head.

The door from the next room opened and Kolpakov walked in. He was pale and kept shaking his head nervously, as though he had swallowed something very bitter; tears were glistening in his eyes.

'What presents did you make me?' Pasha asked, pouncing upon him. 'When did you, allow me to ask you?'

'Presents… that's no matter!' said Kolpakov, and he tossed his head. 'My God! She cried before you, she humbled herself…'

'I am asking you, what presents did you make me?' Pasha cried.

'My God! She, a lady, so proud, so pure… She was ready to go down on her knees to… to this wench! And I've brought her to this! I've allowed it!'

He clutched his head in his hands and moaned.

'No, I shall never forgive myself for this! I shall never forgive myself! Get away from me… you low creature!' he cried with repulsion, backing away from Pasha, and thrusting her off with trembling hands. 'She would have gone down on her knees, and… and to you! Oh, my God!'

He rapidly dressed, and pushing Pasha aside contemptuously, made for the door and went out.

Pasha lay down and began wailing aloud. She was already regretting her things which she had given away so impulsively, and her feelings were hurt. She remembered how three years ago a merchant had beaten her for no sort of reason, and she wailed more loudly than ever.

In the Court

At the district town of N. in the cinnamon-coloured government house in which the Zemstvo, the sessional meetings of the justices of the peace, the Rural Board, the Liquor Board, the Military Board, and many others sit by turns, the Circuit Court was in session on one of the dull days of autumn. Of the above-mentioned cinnamon-coloured house a local official had wittily observed:

'Here is Justitia, here is Policia, here is Militia – a regular boarding school of high-born young ladies.'

But, as the saying is, 'Too many cooks spoil the broth,' and probably that is why the house strikes, oppresses, and overwhelms a fresh unofficial visitor with its dismal barrack-like appearance, its decrepit condition, and the complete absence of any kind of comfort, external or internal. Even on the brightest spring days it seems wrapped in a dense shade, and on clear moonlight nights, when the trees and the little dwelling-houses merged in one blur of shadow seem plunged in quiet slumber, it alone absurdly and inappropriately towers, an oppressive mass of stone, above the modest landscape, spoils the general harmony, and keeps sleepless vigil as though it could not escape from burdensome memories of past unforgiven sins. Inside it is like a barn and extremely unattractive. It is strange to see how readily these elegant lawyers, members of committees, and marshals of nobility, who in their own homes will make a scene over the slightest fume from the stove, or stain on the floor, resign themselves here to whirring ventilation wheels, the disgusting smell of fumigating candles, and the filthy, forever perspiring walls.

The sitting of the circuit court began between nine and ten. The programme of the day was promptly entered upon, with noticeable haste. The cases came on one after another and ended quickly, like a church service without a choir, so that no mind could form a complete picture of all this parti-coloured mass of faces, movements, words, misfortunes, true sayings and lies, all racing by like a river in flood… By two o'clock a great deal had been done: two prisoners had been sentenced to service in convict battalions, one of the privileged class had been sentenced to deprivation of rights and imprisonment, one had been acquitted, one case had been adjourned.

At precisely two o'clock the presiding judge announced that the case 'of the peasant Nikolay Harlamov, charged with the murder of his wife,' would next be heard. The composition of the court remained the same as it had been for the preceding case, except that the place of the defending counsel was filled by a new personage, a beardless young graduate in a coat with bright buttons. The president gave the order – 'Bring in the prisoner!'

But the prisoner, who had been got ready beforehand, was already walking to his bench. He was a tall, thick-set peasant of about fifty-five, completely bald, with an apathetic, hairy face and a big red beard. He was followed by a frail-looking little soldier with a gun.

Just as he was reaching the bench the escort had a trifling mishap. He stumbled and dropped the gun out of his hands, but caught it at once before it touched the ground, knocking his knee violently against the butt end as he did so. A faint laugh was audible in the audience. Either from the pain or perhaps from shame at his awkwardness the soldier flushed a dark red.

After the customary questions to the prisoner, the shuffling of the jury, the calling over and swearing in of the witnesses, the reading of the charge began. The narrow-chested, pale-faced secretary, far too thin for his uniform, and with sticking plaster on his check, read it in a low, thick bass, rapidly like a sacristan, without raising or dropping his voice, as though afraid of exerting his lungs; he was seconded by the ventilation wheel whirring indefatigably behind the judge's table, and the result was a sound that gave a drowsy, narcotic character to the stillness of the hall.

The president, a short-sighted man, not old but with an extremely exhausted face, sat in his armchair without stirring and held his open hand near his brow as though screening his eyes from the sun. To the droning of the ventilation wheel and the secretary he meditated. When the secretary paused for an instant to take breath on beginning a new page, he suddenly started and looked round at the court with lustreless eyes, then bent down to the ear of the judge next to him and asked with a sigh:

'Are you putting up at Demyanov's, Matvey Petrovitch?'

'Yes, at Demyanov's,' answered the other, starting too.

'Next time I shall probably put up there too. It's really impossible to put up at Tipyakov's! There's noise and uproar all night! Knocking, coughing, children crying… It's impossible!'

The assistant prosecutor, a fat, well-nourished, dark man with gold spectacles, with a handsome, well-groomed beard, sat motionless as a statue, with his cheek propped on his fist, reading Byron's 'Cain.' His eyes were full of eager attention and his eyebrows rose higher and higher with wonder… From time to time he dropped back in his chair, gazed without interest straight before him for a minute, and then buried himself in his reading again. The council for the defence moved the blunt end of his pencil about the table and mused with his head on one side… His youthful face expressed nothing but the frigid, immovable boredom which is commonly seen on the face of schoolboys and men on duty who are forced from day to day to sit in the same place, to see the same faces, the same walls. He felt no excitement about the speech he was to make, and indeed what did that speech amount to? On instructions from his superiors in accordance with long-established routine he would fire it off before the jurymen, without passion or ardour, feeling that it was colourless and boring, and then – gallop through the mud and the rain to the station, thence to the town, shortly to receive instructions to go off again to some district to deliver another speech… It was a bore!

At first the prisoner turned pale and coughed nervously into his sleeve, but soon the stillness, the general monotony and boredom infected him too. He looked with dull-witted respectfulness at the judges' uniforms, at the weary faces of the jurymen, and blinked calmly. The surroundings and procedure of the court, the expectation of which had so weighed on his soul while he was awaiting them in prison, now had the most soothing effect on him. What he met here was not at all what he could have expected. The charge of murder hung over him, and yet here he met with neither threatening faces nor indignant looks nor loud phrases about retribution nor sympathy for his extraordinary fate; not one of those who were judging him looked at him with interest or for long… The dingy windows and walls, the voice of the secretary, the attitude of the prosecutor were all saturated with official indifference and produced an atmosphere of frigidity, as though the murderer were simply an official property, or as though he were not being judged by living men, but by some unseen machine, set going, goodness knows how or by whom…

The peasant, reassured, did not understand that the men here were as accustomed to the dramas and tragedies of life and were as blunted by the sight of them as hospital attendants are at the sight of death, and that the whole horror and hopelessness of his position lay just in this mechanical indifference. It seemed that if he were not to sit quietly but to get up and begin beseeching, appealing with tears for their mercy, bitterly repenting, that if he were to die of despair – it would all be shattered against blunted nerves and the callousness of custom, like waves against a rock.

When the secretary finished, the president for some reason passed his hands over the table before him, looked for some time with his eyes screwed up towards the prisoner, and then asked, speaking languidly:

'Prisoner at the bar, do you plead guilty to having murdered your wife on the evening of the ninth of June?'

'No, sir,' answered the prisoner, getting up and holding his gown over his chest.

After this the court proceeded hurriedly to the examination of witnesses. Two peasant women and five men and the village policeman who had made the enquiry were questioned. All of them, mud-bespattered, exhausted with their long walk and waiting in the witnesses' room, gloomy and dispirited, gave the same evidence. They testified that Harlamov lived 'well' with his old woman, like anyone else; that he never beat her except when he had had a drop; that on the ninth of June when the sun was setting the old woman had been found in the porch with her skull broken; that beside her in a pool of blood lay an axe. When they looked for Nikolay to tell him of the calamity he was not in his hut or in the streets. They ran all over the village, looking for him. They went to all the pothouses and huts, but could not find him. He had disappeared, and two days later came of his own accord to the police office, pale, with his clothes torn, trembling all over. He was bound and put in the lock-up.

'Prisoner,' said the president, addressing Harlamov, 'cannot you explain to the court where you were during the three days following the murder?'

'I was wandering about the fields… Neither eating nor drinking…'

'Why did you hide yourself, if it was not you that committed the murder?'

'I was frightened… I was afraid I might be judged guilty…'

'Aha! …Good, sit down!'

The last to be examined was the district doctor who had made a post-mortem on the old woman. He told the court all that he remembered of his report at the post-mortem and all that he had succeeded in thinking of on his way to the court that morning. The president screwed up his eyes at his new glossy black suit, at his foppish cravat, at his moving lips; he listened and in his mind the languid thought seemed to spring up of itself:

'Everyone wears a short jacket nowadays, why has he had his made long? Why long and not short?'

The circumspect creak of boots was audible behind the president's back. It was the assistant prosecutor going up to the table to take some papers.

'Mihail Vladimirovitch,' said the assistant prosecutor, bending down to the president's ear, 'amazingly slovenly the way that Koreisky conducted the investigation. The prisoner's brother was not examined, the village elder was not examined, there's no making anything out of his description of the hut...'

'It can't be helped, it can't be helped,' said the president, sinking back in his chair. 'He's a wreck... dropping to bits!'

'By the way,' whispered the assistant prosecutor, 'look at the audience, in the front row, the third from the right... a face like an actor's... that's the local Croesus. He has a fortune of something like fifty thousand.'

'Really? You wouldn't guess it from his appearance... Well, dear boy, shouldn't we have a break?'

'We will finish the case for the prosecution, and then...'

'As you think best... Well?' the president raised his eyes to the doctor. 'So you consider that death was instantaneous?'

'Yes, in consequence of the extent of the injury to the brain substance...'

When the doctor had finished, the president gazed into the space between the prosecutor and the counsel for the defence and suggested:

'Have you any questions to ask?'

The assistant prosecutor shook his head negatively, without lifting his eyes from 'Cain'; the counsel for the defence unexpectedly stirred and, clearing his throat, asked:

'Tell me, doctor, can you from the dimensions of the wound form any theory as to... as to the mental condition of the criminal? That is, I mean, does the extent of the injury justify the supposition that the accused was suffering from temporary aberration?'

The president raised his drowsy indifferent eyes to the counsel for the defence. The assistant prosecutor tore himself from 'Cain,' and looked at the president. They merely looked, but there was no smile, no surprise, no perplexity-their faces expressed nothing.

'Perhaps,' the doctor hesitated, 'if one considers the force with which... er–er–er... the criminal strikes the blow... However, excuse me, I don't quite understand your question...'

The counsel for the defence did not get an answer to his question, and indeed he did not feel the necessity of one. It was clear even to himself that that question had strayed into his mind and found utterance simply through the effect of the stillness, the boredom, the whirring ventilator wheels.

When they had got rid of the doctor the court rose to examine the 'material evidences'. The first thing examined was the full-skirted coat, upon the sleeve of which there was a dark brownish stain of blood. Harlamov on being questioned as to the origin of the stain stated:

'Three days before my old woman's death Penkov bled his horse. I was there; I was helping to be sure, and… and got smeared with it…'

'But Penkov has just given evidence that he does not remember that you were present at the bleeding…'

'I can't tell about that.'

'Sit down.'

They proceeded to examine the axe with which the old woman had been murdered.

'That's not my axe,' the prisoner declared.

'Whose is it, then?'

'I can't tell… I hadn't an axe…'

'A peasant can't get on for a day without an axe. And your neighbour Ivan Timofeyitch, with whom you mended a sledge, has given evidence that it is your axe…'

'I can't say about that, but I swear before God (Harlamov held out his hand before him and spread out the fingers), before the living God. And I don't remember how long it is since I did have an axe of my own. I did have one like that only a bit smaller, but my son Prohor lost it. Two years before he went into the army, he drove off to fetch wood, got drinking with the fellows, and lost it…'

'Good, sit down.'

This systematic distrust and disinclination to hear him probably irritated and offended Harlamov. He blinked and red patches came out on his cheekbones.

'I swear in the sight of God,' he went on, craning his neck forward. 'If you don't believe me, be pleased to ask my son Prohor. Proshka, what did you do with the axe?' he suddenly asked in a rough voice, turning abruptly to the soldier escorting him. 'Where is it?'

It was a painful moment! Everyone seemed to wince and as it were shrink together. The same fearful, incredible thought flashed like lightning through every head in the court, the thought of possibly fatal coincidence, and not one person in the court dared to look at the soldier's face. Everyone refused to trust his thought and believed that he had heard wrong.

'Prisoner, conversation with the guards is forbidden…' the president made haste to say.

No one saw the escort's face, and horror passed over the hall unseen as in a mask. The usher of the court got up quietly from his place and tiptoeing with his hand held out to balance himself went out of the court. Half a minute later there came the muffled sounds and footsteps that accompany the change of guard.

All raised their heads and, trying to look as though nothing had happened, went on with their work…

Vanka

Vanka Zhukov, a boy of nine, who had been for three months apprenticed to Alyahin the shoemaker, was sitting up on Christmas Eve. Waiting till his master and mistress and their workmen had gone to the midnight service, he took out of his master's cupboard a bottle of ink and a pen with a rusty nib, and, spreading out a crumpled sheet of paper in front of him, began writing. Before forming the first letter he several times looked round fearfully at the door and the windows, stole a glance at the dark ikon, on both sides of which stretched shelves full of lasts, and heaved a broken sigh. The paper lay on the bench while he knelt before it.

'Dear grandfather, Konstantin Makaritch,' he wrote, 'I am writing you a letter. I wish you a happy Christmas, and all blessings from God Almighty. I have neither father nor mother, you are the only one left me.'

Vanka raised his eyes to the dark ikon on which the light of his candle was reflected, and vividly recalled his grandfather, Konstantin Makaritch, who was night watchman to a family called Zhivarev. He was a thin but extraordinarily nimble and lively little old man of sixty-five, with an everlastingly laughing face and drunken eyes. By day he slept in the servants' kitchen, or made jokes with the cooks; at night, wrapped in an ample sheepskin, he walked round the grounds and tapped with his little mallet. Old Kashtanka and Eel, so-called on account of his dark colour and his long body like a weasel's, followed him with hanging heads. This Eel was exceptionally polite and affectionate, and looked with equal kindness on strangers and his own masters, but had not a very good reputation. Under his politeness and meekness was hidden the most Jesuitical cunning. No one knew better how to creep up on occasion and snap at one's legs, to slip into the store-room, or steal a hen from a peasant. His hind legs had been nearly pulled off more than once, twice he had been hanged, every week he was thrashed till he was half dead, but he always revived.

At this moment grandfather was, no doubt, standing at the gate, screwing up his eyes at the red windows of the church, stamping with his high felt boots, and joking with the servants. His little mallet was hanging on his belt. He was clasping his hands, shrugging with the cold, and, with an aged chuckle, pinching first the housemaid, then the cook.

'How about a pinch of snuff?' he was saying, offering the women his snuff-box.

The women would take a sniff and sneeze. Grandfather would be indescribably delighted, go off into a merry chuckle, and cry:

'Tear it off, it has frozen on!'

They give the dogs a sniff of snuff too. Kashtanka sneezes, wriggles her head, and walks away offended. Eel does not sneeze, from politeness, but wags his tail. And the weather is glorious. The air is still, fresh, and transparent. The night is dark, but one can see the whole village with its white roofs and coils of smoke coming from the chimneys, the trees silvered with hoar frost, the snowdrifts. The whole sky spangled with gay twinkling stars, and the Milky Way is as distinct as though it had been washed and rubbed with snow for a holiday…

Vanka sighed, dipped his pen, and went on writing:

'And yesterday I had a wigging. The master pulled me out into the yard by my hair, and whacked me with a boot-stretcher because I accidentally fell asleep while I was rocking their brat in the cradle. And a week ago the mistress told me to clean a herring, and I began from the tail end, and she took the herring and thrust its head in my face. The workmen laugh at me and send me to the tavern for vodka, and tell me to steal the master's cucumbers for them, and the master beats me with anything that comes to hand. And there is nothing to eat. In the morning they give me bread, for dinner, porridge, and in the evening, bread again; but as for tea, or soup, the master and mistress gobble it all up themselves. And I am put to sleep in the passage, and when their wretched brat cries I get no sleep at all, but have to rock the cradle. Dear grandfather, show the divine mercy, take me away from here, home to the village. It's more than I can bear. I bow down to your feet, and will pray to God for you for ever, take me away from here or I shall die.'

Vanka's mouth worked, he rubbed his eyes with his black fist, and gave a sob.

'I will powder your snuff for you,' he went on. 'I will pray for you, and if I do anything you can thrash me like Sidor's goat. And if you think I've no job, then I will beg the steward for Christ's sake to let me clean his boots, or I'll go for a shepherd-boy instead of Fedka. Dear grandfather, it is more than I can bear, it's simply no life at all. I wanted to run away to the village, but I have no boots, and I am afraid of the frost. When I grow up big I will take care of you for this, and not let anyone annoy you, and when you die I will pray for the rest of your soul, just as for my mammy's.

Moscow is a big town. It's all gentlemen's houses, and there are lots of horses, but there are no sheep, and the dogs are not spiteful. The lads here don't go out with the star, and they don't let anyone go into the choir, and once I saw in a shop window fishing-hooks for sale, fitted ready with the line and for all sorts of fish, awfully good ones, there was even one hook that would hold a forty-pound sheat-fish. And I have seen shops where there are guns of all sorts, after the pattern of the master's guns at home, so that I shouldn't wonder if they are a hundred roubles each... And in the butchers' shops there are grouse and woodcocks and fish and hares, but the shopmen don't say where they shoot them.

'Dear grandfather, when they have the Christmas tree at the big house, get me a gilt walnut, and put it away in the green trunk. Ask the young lady Olga Ignatyevna, say it's for Vanka.'

Vanka gave a tremulous sigh, and again stared at the window. He remembered how his grandfather always went into the forest to get the Christmas tree for his master's family, and took his grandson with him. It was a merry time! Grandfather made a noise in his throat, the forest crackled with the frost, and looking at them Vanka chortled too. Before chopping down the Christmas tree, grandfather would smoke a pipe, slowly take a pinch of snuff, and laugh at frozen Vanka... The young fir trees, covered with hoar frost, stood motionless, waiting to see which of them was to die. Wherever one looked, a hare flew like an arrow over the snowdrifts... Grandfather could not refrain from shouting: 'Hold him, hold him... hold him! Ah, the bob-tailed devil!'

When he had cut down the Christmas tree, grandfather used to drag it to the big house, and there set to work to decorate it... The young lady, who was Vanka's favourite, Olga Ignatyevna, was the busiest of all. When Vanka's mother Pelageya was alive, and a servant in the big house, Olga Ignatyevna used to give him goodies, and having nothing better to do, taught him to read and write, to count up to a hundred, and even to dance a quadrille. When Pelageya died, Vanka had been transferred to the servants' kitchen to be with his grandfather, and from the kitchen to the shoemaker's in Moscow.

'Do come, dear grandfather,' Vanka went on with his letter. 'For Christ's sake, I beg you, take me away. Have pity on an unhappy orphan like me; here everyone knocks me about, and I am fearfully hungry; I can't tell you what misery it is, I am always crying. And the other day the master hit me on the head with a last, so that I fell down. My life is wretched, worse than any dog's... I send greetings to Alyona, one-eyed Yegorka, and the coachman, and don't give my concertina to anyone. I remain, your grandson, Ivan Zhukov. Dear grandfather, do come.'

Vanka folded the sheet of writing-paper twice, and put it into an envelope he had bought the day before for a kopeck... After thinking a little, he dipped the pen and wrote the address:

To grandfather in the village.

Then he scratched his head, thought a little, and added: *Konstantin Makaritch.* Glad that he had not been prevented from writing, he put on his cap and, without putting on his little greatcoat, ran out into the street as he was in his shirt…

The shopmen at the butcher's, whom he had questioned the day before, told him that letters were put in post-boxes, and from the boxes were carried about all over the earth in mailcarts with drunken drivers and ringing bells. Vanka ran to the nearest post-box, and thrust the precious letter in the slit…

An hour later, lulled by sweet hopes, he was sound asleep… He dreamed of the stove. On the stove was sitting his grandfather, swinging his bare legs, and reading the letter to the cooks…

By the stove was Eel, wagging his tail.

Champagne: A Wayfarer's Story

In the year in which my story begins I had a job at a little station on one of our southwestern railways. Whether I had a gay or a dull life at the station you can judge from the fact that for fifteen miles round there was not one human habitation, not one woman, not one decent tavern; and in those days I was young, strong, hot-headed, giddy, and foolish. The only distraction I could possibly find was in the windows of the passenger trains, and in the vile vodka which the Jews drugged with thorn-apple. Sometimes there would be a glimpse of a woman's head at a carriage window, and one would stand like a statue without breathing and stare at it until the train turned into an almost invisible speck; or one would drink all one could of the loathsome vodka till one was stupefied and did not feel the passing of the long hours and days. Upon me, a native of the north, the steppe produced the effect of a deserted Tatar cemetery. In the summer the steppe with its solemn calm, the monotonous chur of the grasshoppers, the transparent moon-light from which one could not hide, reduced me to listless melancholy; and in the winter the irreproachable whiteness of the steppe, its cold distance, long nights, and howling wolves oppressed me like a heavy nightmare. There were several people living at the station: my wife and I, a deaf and scrofulous telegraph clerk, and three watchmen. My assistant, a young man who was in consumption, used to go for treatment to the town, where he stayed for months at a time, leaving his duties to me together with the right of pocketing his salary. I had no children, no cake would have tempted visitors to come and see me, and I could only visit other officials on the line, and that no oftener than once a month.

I remember my wife and I saw the New Year in. We sat at table, chewed lazily, and heard the deaf telegraph clerk monotonously tapping on his apparatus in the next room. I had already drunk five glasses of drugged vodka, and, propping my heavy head on my fist, thought of my overpowering boredom from which there was no escape, while my wife sat beside me and did not take her eyes off me. She looked at me as no one can look but a woman who has nothing in this world but a handsome husband. She loved me madly, slavishly, and not merely my good looks, or my soul, but my sins, my ill-humor and boredom, and even my cruelty when, in drunken fury, not knowing how to vent my ill-humor, I tormented her with reproaches.

In spite of the boredom which was consuming me, we were preparing to see the New Year in with exceptional festiveness, and were awaiting midnight with some impatience. The fact is, we had in reserve two bottles of champagne, the real thing, with the label of Veuve Clicquot; this treasure I had won the previous autumn in a bet with the station-master of D. when I was drinking with him at a christening. It sometimes happens during a lesson in mathematics, when the very air is still with boredom, a butterfly flutters into the classroom; the boys toss their heads and begin watching its flight with interest, as though they saw before them not a butterfly but something new and strange; in the same way ordinary champagne, chancing to come into our dreary station, roused us. We sat in silence looking alternately at the clock and at the bottles.

When the hands pointed to five minutes to twelve I slowly began uncorking a bottle. I don't know whether I was affected by the vodka, or whether the bottle was wet, but all I remember is that when the cork flew up to the ceiling with a bang, my bottle slipped out of my hands and fell on the floor. Not more than a glass of the wine was spilt, as I managed to catch the bottle and put my thumb over the foaming neck.

'Well, may the New Year bring you happiness!' I said, filling two glasses. 'Drink!'

My wife took her glass and fixed her frightened eyes on me. Her face was pale and wore a look of horror.

'Did you drop the bottle?' she asked.

'Yes. But what of that?'

'It's unlucky,' she said, putting down her glass and turning paler still. 'It's a bad omen. It means that some misfortune will happen to us this year.'

'What a silly thing you are,' I sighed. 'You are a clever woman, and yet you talk as much nonsense as an old nurse. Drink.'

'God grant it is nonsense, but… something is sure to happen! You'll see.'

She did not even sip her glass, she moved away and sank into thought. I uttered a few stale commonplaces about superstition, drank half a bottle, paced up and down, and then went out of the room.

Outside there was the still frosty night in all its cold, inhospitable beauty. The moon and two white fluffy clouds beside it hung just over the station, motionless as though glued to the spot, and looked as though waiting for something. A faint transparent light came from them and touched the white earth softly, as though afraid of wounding her modesty, and lighted up everything – the snowdrifts, the embankment… It was still.

I walked along the railway embankment.

'Silly woman,' I thought, looking at the sky spangled with brilliant stars. 'Even if one admits that omens sometimes tell the truth, what evil can happen to us? The misfortunes we have endured already, and which are facing us now, are so great that it is difficult to imagine anything worse. What further harm can you do a fish which has been caught and fried and served up with sauce?'

A poplar covered with hoar frost looked in the bluish darkness like a giant wrapt in a shroud. It looked at me sullenly and dejectedly, as though like me it realized its loneliness. I stood a long while looking at it.

'My youth is thrown away for nothing, like a useless cigarette end,' I went on musing. 'My parents died when I was a little child; I was expelled from the high school, I was born of a noble family, but I have received neither education nor breeding, and I have no more knowledge than the humblest mechanic. I have no refuge, no relations, no friends, no work I like. I am not fitted for anything, and in the prime of my powers I am good for nothing but to be stuffed into this little station; I have known nothing but trouble and failure all my life. What can happen worse?'

Red lights came into sight in the distance. A train was moving towards me. The slumbering steppe listened to the sound of it. My thoughts were so bitter that it seemed to me that I was thinking aloud and that the moan of the telegraph wire and the rumble of the train were expressing my thoughts.

'What can happen worse? The loss of my wife?' I wondered. 'Even that is not terrible. It's no good hiding it from my conscience: I don't love my wife. I married her when I was only a wretched boy; now I am young and vigorous, and she has gone off and grown older and sillier, stuffed from her head to her heels with conventional ideas. What charm is there in her maudlin love, in her hollow chest, in her luster-less eyes? I put up with her, but I don't love her. What can happen? My youth is being wasted, as the saying is, for a pinch of snuff. Women flit before my eyes only in the carriage windows, like falling stars. Love I never had and have not. My manhood, my courage, my power of feeling are going to ruin… Everything is being thrown away like dirt, and all my wealth here in the steppe is not worth a farthing.'

The train rushed past me with a roar and indifferently cast the glow of its red lights upon me. I saw it stop by the green lights of the station, stop for a minute and rumble off again. After walking a mile and a half I went back. Melancholy thoughts haunted me still. Painful as it was to me, yet I remember I tried as it were to make my thoughts still gloomier and more melancholy. You know people who are vain and not very clever have moments when the consciousness that they are miserable affords them positive satisfaction, and they even coquet with their misery for their own entertainment. There was a great deal of truth in what I thought, but there was also a great deal that was absurd and conceited, and there was something boyishly defiant in my question: 'What could happen worse?'

'And what is there to happen?' I asked myself. 'I think I have endured everything. I've been ill, I've lost money, I get reprimanded by my superiors every day, and I go hungry, and a mad wolf has run into the station yard. What more is there? I have been insulted, humiliated,… and I have insulted others in my time. I have not been a criminal, it is true, but I don't think I am capable of crime – I am not afraid of being hauled up for it.'

The two little clouds had moved away from the moon and stood at a little distance, looking as though they were whispering about something which the moon must not know. A light breeze was racing across the steppe, bringing the faint rumble of the retreating train.

My wife met me at the doorway. Her eyes were laughing gaily and her whole face was beaming with good-humor.

'There is news for you!' she whispered. 'Make haste, go to your room and put on your new coat; we have a visitor.'

'What visitor?'

'Aunt Natalya Petrovna has just come by the train.'

'What Natalya Petrovna?'

'The wife of my uncle Semyon Fyodoritch. You don't know her. She is a very nice, good woman.'

Probably I frowned, for my wife looked grave and whispered rapidly:

'Of course it is queer her having come, but don't be cross, Nikolay, and don't be hard on her. She is unhappy, you know; Uncle Semyon Fyodoritch really is ill-natured and tyrannical, it is difficult to live with him. She says she will only stay three days with us, only till she gets a letter from her brother.'

My wife whispered a great deal more nonsense to me about her despotic uncle; about the weakness of mankind in general and of young wives in particular; about its being our duty to give shelter to all, even great sinners, and so on. Unable to make head or tail of it, I put on my new coat and went to make acquaintance with my 'aunt.'

A little woman with large black eyes was sitting at the table. My table, the gray walls, my roughly-made sofa, everything to the tiniest grain of dust seemed to have grown younger and more cheerful in the presence of this new, young, beautiful, and dissolute creature, who had a most subtle perfume about her. And that our visitor was a lady of easy virtue I could see from her smile, from her scent, from the peculiar way in which she glanced and made play with her eyelashes, from the tone in which she talked with my wife – a respectable woman. There was no need to tell me she had run away from her husband, that her husband was old and despotic, that she was good-natured and lively; I took it all in at the first glance. Indeed, it is doubtful whether there is a man in all Europe who cannot spot at the first glance a woman of a certain temperament.

'I did not know I had such a big nephew!' said my aunt, holding out her hand to me and smiling.

'And I did not know I had such a pretty aunt,' I answered.

Supper began over again. The cork flew with a bang out of the second bottle, and my aunt swallowed half a glassful at a gulp, and when my wife went out of the room for a moment my aunt did not scruple to drain a full glass. I was drunk both with the wine and with the presence of a woman. Do you remember the song?

> **'Eyes black as pitch, eyes full of passion,**
> **Eyes burning bright and beautiful,**
> **How I love you,**
> **How I fear you!'**

I don't remember what happened next. Anyone who wants to know how love begins may read novels and long stories; I will put it shortly and in the words of the same silly song:

> **'It was an evil hour**
> **When first I met you.'**

Everything went head over heels to the devil. I remember a fearful, frantic whirlwind which sent me flying round like a feather. It lasted a long while, and swept from the face of the earth my wife and my aunt herself and my strength. From the little station in the steppe it has flung me, as you see, into this dark street.

Now tell me what further evil can happen to me?

Darkness

A young peasant, with white eyebrows and eyelashes and broad cheekbones, in a torn sheepskin and big black felt overboots, waited till the Zemstvo doctor had finished seeing his patients and came out to go home from the hospital; then he went up to him, diffidently.

'Please, your honour,' he said.

'What do you want?'

The young man passed the palm of his hand up and over his nose, looked at the sky, and then answered:

'Please, your honour... You've got my brother Vaska the blacksmith from Varvarino in the convict ward here, your honour...'

'Yes, what then?'

'I am Vaska's brother, you see... Father has the two of us: him, Vaska, and me, Kirila; besides us there are three sisters, and Vaska's a married man with a little one... There are a lot of us and no one to work... In the smithy it's nearly two years now since the forge has been heated. I am at the cotton factory, I can't do smith's work, and how can father work? Let alone work, he can't eat properly, he can't lift the spoon to his mouth.'

'What do you want from me?'

'Be merciful! Let Vaska go!'

The doctor looked wonderingly at Kirila, and without saying a word walked on. The young peasant ran on in front and flung himself in a heap at his feet.

'Doctor, kind gentleman!' he besought him, blinking and again passing his open hand over his nose. 'Show heavenly mercy; let Vaska go home! We shall remember you in our prayers for ever! Your honour, let him go! They are all starving! Mother's wailing day in, day out, Vaska's wife's wailing… it's worse than death! I don't care to look upon the light of day. Be merciful; let him go, kind gentleman!'

'Are you stupid or out of your senses?' asked the doctor angrily. 'How can I let him go? Why, he is a convict.'

Kirila began crying. 'Let him go!'

'Tfoo, queer fellow! What right have I? Am I a gaoler or what? They brought him to the hospital for me to treat him, but I have as much right to let him out as I have to put you in prison, silly fellow!

'But they have shut him up for nothing! He was in prison a year before the trial, and now there is no saying what he is there for. It would have been a different thing if he had murdered someone, let us say, or stolen horses; but as it is, what is it all about?'

'Very likely, but how do I come in?'

'They shut a man up and they don't know themselves what for. He was drunk, your honour, did not know what he was doing, and even hit father on the ear and scratched his own cheek on a branch, and two of our fellows – they wanted some Turkish tobacco, you see – began telling him to go with them and break into the Armenian's shop at night for tobacco. Being drunk, he obeyed them, the fool. They broke the lock, you know, got in, and did no end of mischief; they turned everything upside down, broke the windows, and scattered the flour about. They were drunk, that is all one can say! Well, the constable turned up… and with one thing and another they took them off to the magistrate. They have been a whole year in prison, and a week ago, on the Wednesday, they were all three tried in the town. A soldier stood behind them with a gun… people were sworn in. Vaska was less to blame than any, but the gentry decided that he was the ringleader. The other two lads were sent to prison, but Vaska to a convict battalion for three years. And what for? One should judge like a Christian!'

'I have nothing to do with it, I tell you again. Go to the authorities.'

'I have been already! I've been to the court; I have tried to send in a petition – they wouldn't take a petition; I have been to the police captain, and I have been to the examining magistrate, and everyone says, 'It is not my business!' Whose business is it, then? But there is no one above you here in the hospital; you do what you like, your honour.'

'You simpleton,' sighed the doctor, 'once the jury have found him guilty, not the governor, not even the minister, could do anything, let alone the police captain. It's no good your trying to do anything!'

'And who judged him, then?'

'The gentlemen of the jury…'

'They weren't gentlemen, they were our peasants! Andrey Guryev was one; Aloshka Huk was one.'

'Well, I am cold talking to you…'

The doctor waved his hand and walked quickly to his own door. Kirila was on the point of following him, but, seeing the door slam, he stopped.

For ten minutes he stood motionless in the middle of the hospital yard, and without putting on his cap stared at the doctor's house, then he heaved a deep sigh, slowly scratched himself, and walked towards the gate.

'To whom am I to go?' he muttered as he came out on to the road. 'One says it is not his business, another says it is not his business. Whose business is it, then? No, till you grease their hands you will get nothing out of them. The doctor says that, but he keeps looking all the while at my fist to see whether I am going to give him a blue note. Well, brother, I'll go, if it has to be to the governor.'

Shifting from one foot to the other and continually looking round him in an objectless way, he trudged lazily along the road and was apparently wondering where to go… It was not cold and the snow faintly crunched under his feet. Not more than half a mile in front of him the wretched little district town in which his brother had just been tried lay outstretched on the hill. On the right was the dark prison with its red roof and sentry-boxes at the corners; on the left was the big town copse, now covered with hoar-frost. It was still; only an old man, wearing a woman's short jacket and a huge cap, was walking ahead, coughing and shouting to a cow which he was driving to the town.

'Good-day, grandfather,' said Kirila, overtaking him.

'Good-day…'

'Are you driving it to the market?'

'No,' the old man answered lazily.

'Are you a townsman?'

They got into conversation; Kirila told him what he had come to the hospital for, and what he had been talking about to the doctor.

'The doctor does not know anything about such matters, that is a sure thing,' the old man said to him as they were both entering the town; 'though he is a gentleman, he is only taught to cure by every means, but to give you real advice, or, let us say, write out a petition for you – that he cannot do. There are special authorities to do that. You have been to the justice of the peace and to the police captain – they are no good for your business either.'

'Where am I to go?'

'The permanent member of the rural board is the chief person for peasants' affairs. Go to him, Mr. Sineokov.'

'The one who is at Zolotovo?'

'Why, yes, at Zolotovo. He is your chief man. If it is anything that has to do with you peasants even the police captain has no authority against him.'

'It's a long way to go, old man… I dare say it's twelve miles and may be more.'

'One who needs something will go seventy.'

'That is so… Should I send in a petition to him, or what?'

'You will find out there. If you should have a petition the clerk will write you one quick enough. The permanent member has a clerk.'

After parting from the old man Kirila stood still in the middle of the square, thought a little, and walked back out of the town. He made up his mind to go to Zolotovo.

Five days later, as the doctor was on his way home after seeing his patients, he caught sight of Kirila again in his yard. This time the young peasant was not alone, but with a gaunt, very pale old man who nodded his head without ceasing, like a pendulum, and mumbled with his lips.

'Your honour, I have come again to ask your gracious mercy,' began Kirila. 'Here I have come with my father. Be merciful, let Vaska go! The permanent member would not talk to me. He said: 'Go away!' '

'Your honour,' the old man hissed in his throat, raising his twitching eyebrows, 'be merciful! We are poor people, we cannot repay your honour, but if you graciously please, Kiryushka or Vaska can repay you in work. Let them work.'

'We will pay with work,' said Kirila, and he raised his hand above his head as though he would take an oath. 'Let him go! They are starving, they are crying day and night, your honour!'

The young peasant bent a rapid glance on his father, pulled him by the sleeve, and both of them, as at the word of command, fell at the doctor's feet. The latter waved his hand in despair, and, without looking round, walked quickly in at his door.

Home

'**S**omeone came from the Grigoryevs' to fetch a book, but I said you were not at home. The postman brought the newspaper and two letters. By the way, Yevgeny Petrovitch, I should like to ask you to speak to Seryozha. Today, and the day before yesterday, I have noticed that he is smoking. When I began to expostulate with him, he put his fingers in his ears as usual, and sang loudly to drown my voice.'

Yevgeny Petrovitch Bykovsky, the prosecutor of the circuit court, who had just come back from a session and was taking off his gloves in his study, looked at the governess as she made her report, and laughed.

'Seryozha smoking…' he said, shrugging his shoulders. 'I can picture the little cherub with a cigarette in his mouth! Why, how old is he?'

'Seven. You think it is not important, but at his age smoking is a bad and pernicious habit, and bad habits ought to be eradicated in the beginning.'

'Perfectly true. And where does he get the tobacco?'

'He takes it from the drawer in your table.'

'Yes? In that case, send him to me.'

When the governess had gone out, Bykovsky sat down in an arm-chair before his writing-table, shut his eyes, and fell to thinking. He pictured his Seryozha with a huge cigar, a yard long, in the midst of clouds of tobacco smoke, and this caricature made him smile; at the same time, the grave, troubled face of the governess called up memories of the long past, half-forgotten time when smoking aroused in his teachers and parents a strange, not quite intelligible horror. It really was horror. Children were mercilessly flogged and expelled from school, and their lives were made a misery on account of smoking, though not a single teacher or father knew exactly what was the harm or sinfulness of smoking. Even very intelligent people did not scruple to wage war on a vice which they did not understand. Yevgeny Petrovitch remembered the head-master of the high school, a very cultured and good-natured old man, who was so appalled when he found a high-school boy with a cigarette in his mouth that he turned pale, immediately summoned an emergency committee of the teachers, and sentenced the sinner to expulsion. This was probably a law of social life: the less an evil was understood, the more fiercely and coarsely it was attacked.

The prosecutor remembered two or three boys who had been expelled and their subsequent life, and could not help thinking that very often the punishment did a great deal more harm than the crime itself. The living organism has the power of rapidly adapting itself, growing accustomed and inured to any atmosphere whatever, otherwise man would be bound to feel at every moment what an irrational basis there often is underlying his rational activity, and how little of established truth and certainty there is even in work so responsible and so terrible in its effects as that of the teacher, of the lawyer, of the writer…

And such light and discursive thoughts as visit the brain only when it is weary and resting began straying through Yevgeny Petrovitch's head; there is no telling whence and why they come, they do not remain long in the mind, but seem to glide over its surface without sinking deeply into it. For people who are forced for whole hours, and even days, to think by routine in one direction, such free private thinking affords a kind of comfort, an agreeable solace.

It was between eight and nine o'clock in the evening. Overhead, on the second storey, someone was walking up and down, and on the floor above that four hands were playing scales. The pacing of the man overhead who, to judge from his nervous step, was thinking of something harassing, or was suffering from toothache, and the monotonous scales gave the stillness of the evening a drowsiness that disposed to lazy reveries. In the nursery, two rooms away, the governess and Seryozha were talking.

'Pa-pa has come!' carolled the child. 'Papa has co-ome. Pa! Pa! Pa!'

'*Votre père vous appelle, allez vite!*' cried the governess, shrill as a frightened bird. 'I am speaking to you!'

'What am I to say to him, though?' Yevgeny Petrovitch wondered.

But before he had time to think of anything whatever his son Seryozha, a boy of seven, walked into the study.

He was a child whose sex could only have been guessed from his dress: weakly, white-faced, and fragile. He was limp like a hot-house plant, and everything about him seemed extraordinarily soft and tender: his movements, his curly hair, the look in his eyes, his velvet jacket.

'Good evening, papa!' he said, in a soft voice, clambering on to his father's knee and giving him a rapid kiss on his neck. 'Did you send for me?'

'Excuse me, Sergey Yevgenitch,' answered the prosecutor, removing him from his knee. 'Before kissing we must have a talk, and a serious talk… I am angry with you, and don't love you any more. I tell you, my boy, I don't love you, and you are no son of mine…'

Seryozha looked intently at his father, then shifted his eyes to the table, and shrugged his shoulders.

'What have I done to you?' he asked in perplexity, blinking. 'I haven't been in your study all day, and I haven't touched anything.'

'Natalya Semyonovna has just been complaining to me that you have been smoking… Is it true? Have you been smoking?'

'Yes, I did smoke once… That's true…'

'Now you see you are lying as well,' said the prosecutor, frowning to disguise a smile. 'Natalya Semyonovna has seen you smoking twice. So you see you have been detected in three misdeeds: smoking, taking someone else's tobacco, and lying. Three faults.'

'Oh yes,' Seryozha recollected, and his eyes smiled. 'That's true, that's true; I smoked twice: today and before.'

'So you see it was not once, but twice… I am very, very much displeased with you! You used to be a good boy, but now I see you are spoilt and have become a bad one.'

Yevgeny Petrovitch smoothed down Seryozha's collar and thought: 'What more am I to say to him!'

'Yes, it's not right,' he continued. 'I did not expect it of you. In the first place, you ought not to take tobacco that does not belong to you. Every person has only the right to make use of his own property; if he takes anyone else's… he is a bad man!' ('I am not saying the right thing!' thought Yevgeny Petrovitch.) 'For instance, Natalya Semyonovna has a box with her clothes in it. That's her box, and we – that is, you and I – dare not touch it, as it is not ours. That's right, isn't it? You've got toy horses and pictures… I don't take them, do I? Perhaps I might like to take them, but… they are not mine, but yours!'

'Take them if you like!' said Seryozha, raising his eyebrows. 'Please don't hesitate, papa, take them! That yellow dog on your table is mine, but I don't mind… Let it stay.'

'You don't understand me,' said Bykovsky. 'You have given me the dog, it is mine now and I can do what I like with it; but I didn't give you the tobacco! The tobacco is mine.' ('I am not explaining properly!' thought the prosecutor. 'It's wrong! Quite wrong!') 'If I want to smoke someone else's tobacco, I must first of all ask his permission…'

Languidly linking one phrase on to another and imitating the language of the nursery, Bykovsky tried to explain to his son the meaning of property. Seryozha gazed at his chest and listened attentively (he liked talking to his father in the evening), then he leaned his elbow on the edge of the table and began screwing up his short-sighted eyes at the papers and the inkstand. His eyes strayed over the table and rested on the gum-bottle.

'Papa, what is gum made of?' he asked suddenly, putting the bottle to his eyes.

Bykovsky took the bottle out of his hands and set it in its place and went on:

'Secondly, you smoke… That's very bad. Though I smoke it does not follow that you may. I smoke and know that it is stupid, I blame myself and don't like myself for it.' ('A clever teacher, I am!' he thought.) 'Tobacco is very bad for the health, and anyone who smokes dies earlier than he should. It's particularly bad for boys like you to smoke. Your chest is weak, you haven't reached your full strength yet, and smoking leads to consumption and other illness in weak people. Uncle Ignat died of consumption, you know. If he hadn't smoked, perhaps he would have lived till now.'

Seryozha looked pensively at the lamp, touched the lamp-shade with his finger, and heaved a sigh.

'Uncle Ignat played the violin splendidly!' he said. 'His violin is at the Grigoryevs' now.'

Seryozha leaned his elbows on the edge of the table again, and sank into thought. His white face wore a fixed expression, as though he were listening or following a train of thought of his own; distress and something like fear came into his big staring eyes. He was most likely thinking now of death, which had so lately carried off his mother and Uncle Ignat. Death carries mothers and uncles off to the other world, while their children and violins remain upon the earth. The dead live somewhere in the sky beside the stars, and look down from there upon the earth. Can they endure the parting?

'What am I to say to him?' thought Yevgeny Petrovitch. 'He's not listening to me. Obviously he does not regard either his misdoings or my arguments as serious. How am I to drive it home?'

The prosecutor got up and walked about the study.

'Formerly, in my time, these questions were very simply settled,' he reflected. 'Every urchin who was caught smoking was thrashed. The cowardly and faint-hearted did actually give up smoking, any who were somewhat more plucky and intelligent, after the thrashing took to carrying tobacco in the legs of their boots, and smoking in the barn. When they were caught in the barn and thrashed again, they would go away to smoke by the river… and so on, till the boy grew up. My mother used to give me money and sweets not to smoke. Now that method is looked upon as worthless and immoral. The modern teacher, taking his stand on logic, tries to make the child form good principles, not from fear, nor from desire for distinction or reward, but consciously.'

While he was walking about, thinking, Seryozha climbed up with his legs on a chair sideways to the table, and began drawing. That he might not spoil official paper nor touch the ink, a heap of half-sheets, cut on purpose for him, lay on the table together with a blue pencil.

'Cook was chopping up cabbage today and she cut her finger,' he said, drawing a little house and moving his eyebrows. 'She gave such a scream that we were all frightened and ran into the kitchen. Stupid thing! Natalya Semyonovna told her to dip her finger in cold water, but she sucked it... And how could she put a dirty finger in her mouth! That's not proper, you know, papa!'

Then he went on to describe how, while they were having dinner, a man with a hurdy-gurdy had come into the yard with a little girl, who had danced and sung to the music.

'He has his own train of thought!' thought the prosecutor. 'He has a little world of his own in his head, and he has his own ideas of what is important and unimportant. To gain possession of his attention, it's not enough to imitate his language, one must also be able to think in the way he does. He would understand me perfectly if I really were sorry for the loss of the tobacco, if I felt injured and cried... That's why no one can take the place of a mother in bringing up a child, because she can feel, cry, and laugh together with the child. One can do nothing by logic and morality. What more shall I say to him? What?'

And it struck Yevgeny Petrovitch as strange and absurd that he, an experienced advocate, who spent half his life in the practice of reducing people to silence, forestalling what they had to say, and punishing them, was completely at a loss and did not know what to say to the boy.

'I say, give me your word of honour that you won't smoke again,' he said.

'Word of hon-nour!' carolled Seryozha, pressing hard on the pencil and bending over the drawing. 'Word of hon-nour!'

'Does he know what is meant by word of honour?' Bykovsky asked himself. 'No, I am a poor teacher of morality! If some schoolmaster or one of our legal fellows could peep into my brain at this moment he would call me a poor stick, and would very likely suspect me of unnecessary subtlety… But in school and in court, of course, all these wretched questions are far more simply settled than at home; here one has to do with people whom one loves beyond everything, and love is exacting and complicates the question. If this boy were not my son, but my pupil, or a prisoner on his trial, I should not be so cowardly, and my thoughts would not be racing all over the place!'

Yevgeny Petrovitch sat down to the table and pulled one of Seryozha's drawings to him. In it there was a house with a crooked roof, and smoke which came out of the chimney like a flash of lightning in zigzags up to the very edge of the paper; beside the house stood a soldier with dots for eyes and a bayonet that looked like the figure 4.

'A man can't be taller than a house,' said the prosecutor.

Seryozha got on his knee, and moved about for some time to get comfortably settled there.

'No, papa!' he said, looking at his drawing. 'If you were to draw the soldier small you would not see his eyes.'

Ought he to argue with him? From daily observation of his son the prosecutor had become convinced that children, like savages, have their own artistic standpoints and requirements peculiar to them, beyond the grasp of grown-up people. Had he been attentively observed, Seryozha might have struck a grown-up person as abnormal. He thought it possible and reasonable to draw men taller than houses, and to represent in pencil, not only objects, but even his sensations. Thus he would depict the sounds of an orchestra in the form of smoke like spherical blurs, a whistle in the form of a spiral thread… To his mind sound was closely connected with form and colour, so that when he painted letters he invariably painted the letter L yellow, M red, A black, and so on.

Abandoning his drawing, Seryozha shifted about once more, got into a comfortable attitude, and busied himself with his father's beard. First he carefully smoothed it, then he parted it and began combing it into the shape of whiskers.

'Now you are like Ivan Stepanovitch,' he said, 'and in a minute you will be like our porter. Papa, why is it porters stand by doors? Is it to prevent thieves getting in?'

The prosecutor felt the child's breathing on his face, he was continually touching his hair with his cheek, and there was a warm soft feeling in his soul, as soft as though not only his hands but his whole soul were lying on the velvet of Seryozha's jacket.

He looked at the boy's big dark eyes, and it seemed to him as though from those wide pupils there looked out at him his mother and his wife and everything that he had ever loved.

'To think of thrashing him…' he mused. 'A nice task to devise a punishment for him! How can we undertake to bring up the young? In old days people were simpler and thought less, and so settled problems boldly. But we think too much, we are eaten up by logic… The more developed a man is, the more he reflects and gives himself up to subtleties, the more undecided and scrupulous he becomes, and the more timidity he shows in taking action. How much courage and self-confidence it needs, when one comes to look into it closely, to undertake to teach, to judge, to write a thick book…'

It struck ten.

'Come, boy, it's bedtime,' said the prosecutor. 'Say goodnight and go.'

'No, papa,' said Seryozha, 'I will stay a little longer. Tell me something! Tell me a story…'

'Very well, only after the story you must go to bed at once.'

Yevgeny Petrovitch on his free evenings was in the habit of telling Seryozha stories. Like most people engaged in practical affairs, he did not know a single poem by heart, and could not remember a single fairy tale, so he had to improvise. As a rule he began with the stereotyped: 'In a certain country, in a certain kingdom,' then he heaped up all kinds of innocent nonsense and had no notion as he told the beginning how the story would go on, and how it would end. Scenes, characters, and situations were taken at random, impromptu, and the plot and the moral came of itself as it were, with no plan on the part of the story-teller. Seryozha was very fond of this improvisation, and the prosecutor noticed that the simpler and the less ingenious the plot, the stronger the impression it made on the child.

'Listen,' he said, raising his eyes to the ceiling. 'Once upon a time, in a certain country, in a certain kingdom, there lived an old, very old emperor with a long grey beard, and… and with great grey moustaches like this. Well, he lived in a glass palace which sparkled and glittered in the sun, like a great piece of clear ice. The palace, my boy, stood in a huge garden, in which there grew oranges, you know… bergamots, cherries… tulips, roses, and lilies-of-the-valley were in flower in it, and birds of different colours sang there… Yes… On the trees there hung little glass bells, and, when the wind blew, they rang so sweetly that one was never tired of hearing them. Glass gives a softer, tenderer note than metals… Well, what next? There were fountains in the garden… Do you remember you saw a fountain at Auntie Sonya's summer villa? Well, there were fountains just like that in the emperor's garden, only ever so much bigger, and the jets of water reached to the top of the highest poplar.'

Yevgeny Petrovitch thought a moment, and went on:

'The old emperor had an only son and heir of his kingdom – a boy as little as you. He was a good boy. He was never naughty, he went to bed early, he never touched anything on the table, and altogether he was a sensible boy. He had only one fault, he used to smoke…'

Seryozha listened attentively, and looked into his father's eyes without blinking. The prosecutor went on, thinking: 'What next?' He spun out a long rigmarole, and ended like this:

'The emperor's son fell ill with consumption through smoking, and died when he was twenty. His infirm and sick old father was left without anyone to help him. There was no one to govern the kingdom and defend the palace. Enemies came, killed the old man, and destroyed the palace, and now there are neither cherries, nor birds, nor little bells in the garden… That's what happened.'

This ending struck Yevgeny Petrovitch as absurd and naïve, but the whole story made an intense impression on Seryozha. Again his eyes were clouded by mournfulness and something like fear; for a minute he looked pensively at the dark window, shuddered, and said, in a sinking voice:

'I am not going to smoke any more…'

When he had said good-night and gone away his father walked up and down the room and smiled to himself.

'They would tell me it was the influence of beauty, artistic form,' he meditated. 'It may be so, but that's no comfort. It's not the right way, all the same... Why must morality and truth never be offered in their crude form, but only with embellishments, sweetened and gilded like pills? It's not normal... It's falsification... deception... tricks ...'

He thought of the jurymen to whom it was absolutely necessary to make a 'speech,' of the general public who absorb history only from legends and historical novels, and of himself and how he had gathered an understanding of life not from sermons and laws, but from fables, novels, poems.

'Medicine should be sweet, truth beautiful, and man has had this foolish habit since the days of Adam... though, indeed, perhaps it is all natural, and ought to be so... There are many deceptions and delusions in nature that serve a purpose.'

He set to work, but lazy, intimate thoughts still strayed through his mind for a good while. Overhead the scales could no longer be heard, but the inhabitant of the second storey was still pacing from one end of the room to another.

A Play

'**P**avel Vassilyevitch, there's a lady here, asking for you,' Luka announced. 'She's been waiting a good hour...'

Pavel Vassilyevitch had only just finished lunch. Hearing of the lady, he frowned and said:

'Oh, damn her! Tell her I'm busy.'

'She has been here five times already, Pavel Vassilyevitch. She says she really must see you... She's almost crying.'

'H'm... very well, then, ask her into the study.'

Without haste Pavel Vassilyevitch put on his coat, took a pen in one hand, and a book in the other, and trying to look as though he were very busy he went into the study. There the visitor was awaiting him – a large stout lady with a red, beefy face, in spectacles. She looked very respectable, and her dress was more than fashionable (she had on a crinolette of four storeys and a high hat with a reddish bird in it). On seeing him she turned up her eyes and folded her hands in supplication.

'You don't remember me, of course,' she began in a high masculine tenor, visibly agitated. ' I… I have had the pleasure of meeting you at the Hrutskys… I am Mme. Murashkin…'

'A… a… a… h'm… Sit down! What can I do for you?'

'You… you see… I… I…' the lady went on, sitting down and becoming still more agitated. 'You don't remember me… I'm Mme. Murashkin… You see I'm a great admirer of your talent and always read your articles with great enjoyment… Don't imagine I'm flattering you – God forbid! – I'm only giving honour where honour is due… I am always reading you… always! To some extent I am myself not a stranger to literature – that is, of course… I will not venture to call myself an authoress, but… still I have added my little quota… I have published at different times three stories for children… You have not read them, of course… I have translated a good deal and… and my late brother used to write for *The Cause*.'

'To be sure… er – er – er — What can I do for you?'

'You see… (the lady cast down her eyes and turned redder) I know your talents… your views, Pavel Vassilyevitch, and I have been longing to learn your opinion, or more exactly… to ask your advice. I must tell you I have perpetrated a play, my first-born – *pardon pour l'expression!* – and before sending it to the Censor I should like above all things to have your opinion on it.'

Nervously, with the flutter of a captured bird, the lady fumbled in her skirt and drew out a fat manuscript.

Pavel Vassilyevitch liked no articles but his own. When threatened with the necessity of reading other people's, or listening to them, he felt as though he were facing the cannon's mouth. Seeing the manuscript he took fright and hastened to say:

'Very good,… leave it,… I'll read it.'

'Pavel Vassilyevitch,' the lady said languishingly, clasping her hands and raising them in supplication, 'I know you're busy… Your every minute is precious, and I know you're inwardly cursing me at this moment, but… Be kind, allow me to read you my play… Do be so very sweet!'

'I should be delighted…' faltered Pavel Vassilyevitch; 'but, Madam, I'm… I'm very busy… I'm… I'm obliged to set off this minute.'

'Pavel Vassilyevitch,' moaned the lady and her eyes filled with tears,

'I'm asking a sacrifice! I am insolent, I am intrusive, but be magnanimous. Tomorrow I'm leaving for Kazan and I should like to know your opinion today. Grant me half an hour of your attention… only one half-hour… I implore you!

Pavel Vassilyevitch was cotton-wool at core, and could not refuse. When it seemed to him that the lady was about to burst into sobs and fall on her knees, he was overcome with confusion and muttered helplessly.

'Very well; certainly… I will listen… I will give you half an hour.'

The lady uttered a shriek of joy, took off her hat and settling herself, began to read. At first she read a scene in which a footman and a house maid, tidying up a sumptuous drawing-room, talked at length about their young lady, Anna Sergyevna, who was building a school and a hospital in the village. When the footman had left the room, the maid-servant pronounced a monologue to the effect that education is light and ignorance is darkness; then Mme. Murashkin brought the footman back into the drawing-room and set him uttering a long monologue concerning his master, the General, who disliked his daughter's views, intended to marry her to a rich *kammer junker,* and held that the salvation of the people lay in unadulterated ignorance. Then, when the servants had left the stage, the young lady herself appeared and informed the audience that she had not slept all night, but had been thinking of Valentin Ivanovitch, who was the son of a poor teacher and assisted his sick father gratuitously. Valentin had studied all the sciences, but had no faith in friendship nor in love; he had no object in life and longed for death, and therefore she, the young lady, must save him.

Pavel Vassilyevitch listened, and thought with yearning anguish of his sofa. He scanned the lady viciously, felt her masculine tenor thumping on his eardrums, understood nothing, and thought:

'The devil sent you… as though I wanted to listen to your tosh! It's not my fault you've written a play, is it? My God! what a thick manuscript! What an infliction!'

Pavel Vassilyevitch glanced at the wall where the portrait of his wife was hanging and remembered that his wife had asked him to buy and bring to their summer cottage five yards of tape, a pound of cheese, and some tooth-powder.

'I hope I've not lost the pattern of that tape,' he thought, 'where did I put it? I believe it's in my blue reefer jacket… Those wretched flies have covered her portrait with spots already, I must tell Olga to wash the glass… She's reading the twelfth scene, so we must soon be at the end of the first act. As though inspiration were possible in this heat and with such a mountain of flesh, too! Instead of writing plays she'd much better eat cold vinegar hash and sleep in a cellar…'

'You don't think that monologue's a little too long?' the lady asked suddenly, raising her eyes.

Pavel Vassilyevitch had not heard the monologue, and said in a voice as guilty as though not the lady but he had written that monologue:

'No, no, not at all. It's very nice…'

The lady beamed with happiness and continued reading:

ANNA: You are consumed by analysis. Too early you have ceased to live in the heart and have put your faith in the intellect.

VALENTIN: What do you mean by the heart? That is a concept of anatomy. As a conventional term for what are called the feelings, I do not admit it.

ANNA (*confused*): And love? Surely that is not merely a product of the association of ideas? Tell me frankly, have you ever loved?

VALENTIN (*bitterly*): Let us not touch on old wounds not yet healed. (*A pause.*) What are you thinking of?

ANNA: I believe you are unhappy.

During the sixteenth scene Pavel Vassilyevitch yawned, and accidently made with his teeth the sound dogs make when they catch a fly. He was dismayed at this unseemly sound, and to cover it assumed an expression of rapt attention.

'Scene seventeen! When will it end?' he thought. 'Oh, my God! If this torture is prolonged another ten minutes I shall shout for the police. It's insufferable.'

But at last the lady began reading more loudly and more rapidly, and finally raising her voice she read 'Curtain.'

Pavel Vassilyevitch uttered a faint sigh and was about to get up, but the lady promptly turned the page and went on reading:

ACT II. – *Scene, a village street. On right, School. On left, Hospital.* Villagers, *male and female, sitting on the hospital steps.*

'Excuse me,' Pavel Vassilyevitch broke in, 'how many acts are there?'

'Five,' answered the lady, and at once, as though fearing her audience might escape her, she went on rapidly.

VALENTIN *is looking out of the schoolhouse window. In the background* Villagers *can be seen taking their goods to the Inn.*

Like a man condemned to be executed and convinced of the impossibility of a reprieve, Pavel Vassilyevitch gave up expecting the end, abandoned all hope, and simply tried to prevent his eyes from closing, and to retain an expression of attention on his face... The future when the lady would finish her play and depart seemed to him so remote that he did not even think of it.

'Trooo–too–too–too...' the lady's voice sounded in his ears. 'Troo–too–too... sh–sh–sh–sh...'

'I forgot to take my soda,' he thought. 'What am I thinking about? Oh – my soda... Most likely I shall have a bilious attack... It's extraordinary, Smirnovsky swills vodka all day long and yet he never has a bilious attack... There's a bird settled on the window... a sparrow...'

Pavel Vassilyevitch made an effort to unglue his strained and closing eyelids, yawned without opening his mouth, and stared at Mme. Murashkin. She grew misty and swayed before his eyes, turned into a triangle and her head pressed against the ceiling...

VALENTIN No, let me depart.

ANNA (*in dismay*): Why?

VALENTIN (*aside*): She has turned pale! (*To her*) Do not force me to explain. Sooner would I die than you should know the reason.

ANNA (*after a pause*): You cannot go away...

The lady began to swell, swelled to an immense size, and melted into the dingy atmosphere of the study – only her moving mouth was visible; then she suddenly dwindled to the size of a bottle, swayed from side to side, and with the table retreated to the further end of the room...

VALENTIN (*holding* ANNA *in his arms*): You have given me new life! You have shown me an object to live for! You have renewed me as the Spring rain renews the awakened earth! But... it is too late, too late! The ill that gnaws at my heart is beyond cure...

Pavel Vassilyevitch started and with dim and smarting eyes stared at the reading lady; for a minute he gazed fixedly as though understanding nothing…

SCENE XI. – *The same. The* BARON *and the* POLICE INSPECTOR *with assistants.*

VALENTIN: Take me!

ANNA: I am his! Take me too! Yes, take me too! I love him, I love him more than life!

BARON: Anna Sergyevna, you forget that you are ruining your father…

The lady began swelling again… Looking round him wildly Pavel Vassilyevitch got up, yelled in a deep, unnatural voice, snatched from the table a heavy paper-weight, and beside himself, brought it down with all his force on the authoress's head…

'Give me in charge, I've killed her!' he said to the maidservant who ran in, a minute later.

The jury acquitted him.

The Runaway

It had been a long business. At first Pashka had walked with his mother in the rain, at one time across a mown field, then by forest paths, where the yellow leaves stuck to his boots; he had walked until it was daylight. Then he had stood for two hours in the dark passage, waiting for the door to open. It was not so cold and damp in the passage as in the yard, but with the high wind spurts of rain flew in even there. When the passage gradually became packed with people Pashka, squeezed among them, leaned his face against somebody's sheepskin which smelt strongly of salt fish, and sank into a doze. But at last the bolt clicked, the door flew open, and Pashka and his mother went into the waiting-room. All the patients sat on benches without stirring or speaking. Pashka looked round at them, and he too was silent, though he was seeing a great deal that was strange and funny. Only once, when a lad came into the waiting-room hopping on one leg, Pashka longed to hop too; he nudged his mother's elbow, giggled in his sleeve, and said: 'Look, mammy, a sparrow.'

'Hush, child, hush!' said his mother.

A sleepy-looking hospital assistant appeared at the little window. 'Come and be registered!' he boomed out.

All of them, including the funny lad who hopped, filed up to the window. The assistant asked each one his name, and his father's name, where he lived, how long he had been ill, and so on. From his mother's answers, Pashka learned that his name was not Pashka, but Pavel Galaktionov, that he was seven years old, that he could not read or write, and that he had been ill ever since Easter.

Soon after the registration, he had to stand up for a little while; the doctor in a white apron, with a towel round his waist, walked across the waiting-room. As he passed by the boy who hopped, he shrugged his shoulders, and said in a sing-song tenor:

'Well, you are an idiot! Aren't you an idiot? I told you to come on Monday, and you come on Friday. It's nothing to me if you don't come at all, but you know, you idiot, your leg will be done for!'

The lad made a pitiful face, as though he were going to beg for alms, blinked, and said:

'Kindly do something for me, Ivan Mikolaitch!'

'It's no use saying "Ivan Mikolaitch,"' the doctor mimicked him. 'You were told to come on Monday, and you ought to obey. You are an idiot, and that is all about it.'

The doctor began seeing the patients. He sat in his little room, and called up the patients in turn. Sounds were continually coming from the little room, piercing wails, a child's crying, or the doctor's angry words:

'Come, why are you bawling? Am I murdering you, or what? Sit quiet!'

Pashka's turn came.

'Pavel Galaktionov!' shouted the doctor.

His mother was aghast, as though she had not expected this summons, and taking Pashka by the hand, she led him into the room.

The doctor was sitting at the table, mechanically tapping on a thick book with a little hammer.

'What's wrong?' he asked, without looking at them.

'The little lad has an ulcer on his elbow, sir,' answered his mother, and her face assumed an expression as though she really were terribly grieved at Pashka's ulcer.

'Undress him!'

Pashka, panting, unwound the kerchief from his neck, then wiped his nose on his sleeve, and began deliberately pulling off his sheepskin.

'Woman, you have not come here on a visit!' said the doctor angrily. 'Why are you dawdling? You are not the only one here.'

Pashka hurriedly flung the sheepskin on the floor, and with his mother's help took off his shirt…The doctor looked at him lazily, and patted him on his bare stomach.

'You have grown quite a respectable corporation, brother Pashka,' he said, and heaved a sigh. 'Come, show me your elbow.'

Pashka looked sideways at the basin full of bloodstained slops, looked at the doctor's apron, and began to cry.

'May-ay!' the doctor mimicked him. 'Nearly old enough to be married, spoilt boy, and here he is blubbering! For shame!'

Pashka, trying not to cry, looked at his mother, and in that look could be read the entreaty: 'Don't tell them at home that I cried at the hospital.'

The doctor examined his elbow, pressed it, heaved a sigh, clicked with his lips, then pressed it again.

'You ought to be beaten, woman, but there is no one to do it,' he said. 'Why didn't you bring him before? Why, the whole arm is done for. Look, foolish woman. You see, the joint is diseased!'

'You know best, kind sir…' sighed the woman.

'Kind sir… She's let the boy's arm rot, and now it is "kind sir." What kind of workman will he be without an arm? You'll be nursing him and looking after him for ages. I bet if you had had a pimple on your nose, you'd have run to the hospital quick enough, but you have left your boy to rot for six months. You are all like that.'

The doctor lighted a cigarette. While the cigarette smoked, he scolded the woman, and shook his head in time to the song he was humming inwardly, while he thought of something else. Pashka stood naked before him, listening and looking at the smoke. When the cigarette went out, the doctor started, and said in a lower tone:

'Well, listen, woman. You can do nothing with ointments and drops in this case. You must leave him in the hospital.'

'If necessary, sir, why not?'

'We must operate on him. You stop with me, Pashka,' said the doctor, slapping Pashka on the shoulder. 'Let mother go home, and you and I will stop here, old man. It's nice with me, old boy, it's first-rate here. I'll tell you what we'll do, Pashka, we will go catching finches together. I will show you a fox! We will go visiting together! Shall we? And mother will come for you tomorrow! Eh?'

Pashka looked inquiringly at his mother.

'You stay, child!' she said.

'He'll stay, he'll stay!' cried the doctor gleefully. 'And there is no need to discuss it. I'll show him a live fox! We will go to the fair together to buy candy! Marya Denisovna, take him upstairs!'

The doctor, apparently a light-hearted and friendly fellow, seemed glad to have company; Pashka wanted to oblige him, especially as he had never in his life been to a fair, and would have been glad to have a look at a live fox, but how could he do without his mother?

After a little reflection he decided to ask the doctor to let his mother stay in the hospital too, but before he had time to open his mouth the lady assistant was already taking him upstairs. He walked up and looked about him with his mouth open. The staircase, the floors, and the doorposts – everything huge, straight, and bright-were painted a splendid yellow colour, and had a delicious smell of Lenten oil. On all sides lamps were hanging, strips of carpet stretched along the floor, copper taps stuck out on the walls. But best of all Pashka liked the bedstead upon which he was made to sit down, and the grey woollen coverlet. He touched the pillows and the coverlet with his hands, looked round the ward, and made up his mind that it was very nice at the doctor's.

The ward was not a large one, it consisted of only three beds. One bed stood empty, the second was occupied by Pashka, and on the third sat an old man with sour eyes, who kept coughing and spitting into a mug. From Pashka's bed part of another ward could be seen with two beds; on one a very pale wasted-looking man with an india-rubber bottle on his head was asleep; on the other a peasant with his head tied up, looking very like a woman, was sitting with his arms spread out.

After making Pashka sit down, the assistant went out and came back a little later with a bundle of clothes under her arm.

'These are for you,' she said, 'put them on.'

Pashka undressed and, not without satisfaction began attiring himself in his new array. When he had put on the shirt, the drawers, and the little grey dressing-gown, he looked at himself complacently, and thought that it would not be bad to walk through the village in that costume. His imagination pictured his mother's sending him to the kitchen garden by the river to gather cabbage leaves for the little pig; he saw himself walking along, while the boys and girls surrounded him and looked with envy at his little dressing-gown.

A nurse came into the ward, bringing two tin bowls, two spoons, and two pieces of bread. One bowl she set before the old man, the other before Pashka.

'Eat!' she said.

Looking into his bowl, Pashka saw some rich cabbage soup, and in the soup a piece of meat, and thought again that it was very nice at the doctor's, and that the doctor was not nearly so cross as he had seemed at first. He spent a long time swallowing the soup, licking the spoon after each mouthful, then when there was nothing left in the bowl but the meat he stole a look at the old man, and felt envious that he was still eating the soup. With a sigh Pashka attacked the meat, trying to make it last as long as possible, but his efforts were fruitless; the meat, too, quickly vanished. There was nothing left but the piece of bread. Plain bread without anything on it was not appetising, but there was no help for it. Pashka thought a little, and ate the bread. At that moment the nurse came in with another bowl. This time there was roast meat with potatoes in the bowl.

'And where is the bread?' asked the nurse.

Instead of answering, Pashka puffed out his cheeks, and blew out the air.

'Why did you gobble it all up?' said the nurse reproachfully. 'What are you going to eat your meat with?'

She went and fetched another piece of bread. Pashka had never eaten roast meat in his life, and trying it now found it very nice. It vanished quickly, and then he had a piece of bread left bigger than the first. When the old man had finished his dinner, he put away the remains of his bread in a little table. Pashka meant to do the same, but on second thoughts ate his piece.

When he had finished he went for a walk. In the next ward, besides the two he had seen from the door, there were four other people. Of these only one drew his attention. This was a tall, extremely emaciated peasant with a morose-looking, hairy face. He was sitting on the bed, nodding his head and swinging his right arm all the time like a pendulum. Pashka could not take his eyes off him for a long time. At first the man's regular pendulum-like movements seemed to him curious, and he thought they were done for the general amusement, but when he looked into the man's face he felt frightened, and realised that he was terribly ill. Going into a third ward he saw two peasants with dark red faces as though they were smeared with clay. They were sitting motionless on their beds, and with their strange faces, in which it was hard to distinguish their features, they looked like heathen idols.

'Auntie, why do they look like that?' Pashka asked the nurse.

'They have got smallpox, little lad.'

Going back to his own ward, Pashka sat down on his bed and began waiting for the doctor to come and take him to catch finches, or to go to the fair. But the doctor did not come. He got a passing glimpse of a hospital assistant at the door of the next ward. He bent over the patient on whose head lay a bag of ice, and cried: 'Mihailo!'

But the sleeping man did not stir. The assistant made a gesture and went away. Pashka scrutinised the old man, his next neighbour. The old man coughed without ceasing and spat into a mug. His cough had a long-drawn-out, creaking sound.

Pashka liked one peculiarity about him; when he drew the air in as he coughed, something in his chest whistled and sang on different notes.

'Grandfather, what is it whistles in you?' Pashka asked.

The old man made no answer. Pashka waited a little and asked:

'Grandfather, where is the fox?'

'What fox?'

'The live one.'

'Where should it be? In the forest!'

A long time passed, but the doctor still did not appear. The nurse brought in tea, and scolded Pashka for not having saved any bread for his tea; the assistant came once more and set to work to wake Mihailo. It turned blue outside the windows, the wards were lighted up, but the doctor did not appear. It was too late now to go to the fair and catch finches; Pashka stretched himself on his bed and began thinking. He remembered the candy promised him by the doctor, the face and voice of his mother, the darkness in his hut at home, the stove, peevish granny Yegorovna… and he suddenly felt sad and dreary. He remembered that his mother was coming for him next day, smiled, and shut his eyes.

He was awakened by a rustling. In the next ward someone was stepping about and speaking in a whisper. Three figures were moving about Mihailo's bed in the dim light of the night-light and the ikon lamp.

'Shall we take him, bed and all, or without?' asked one of them.

'Without. You won't get through the door with the bed.'

'He's died at the wrong time, the Kingdom of Heaven be his!'

One took Mihailo by his shoulders, another by his legs and lifted him up: Mihailo's arms and the skirt of his dressing-gown hung limply to the ground. A third – it was the peasant who looked like a woman – crossed himself, and all three tramping clumsily with their feet and stepping on Mihailo's skirts, went out of the ward.

There came the whistle and humming on different notes from the chest of the old man who was asleep. Pashka listened, peeped at the dark windows, and jumped out of bed in terror.

'Ma-a-mka!' he moaned in a deep bass.

And without waiting for an answer, he rushed into the next ward. There the darkness was dimly lighted up by a night-light and the ikon lamp; the patients, upset by the death of Mihailo, were sitting on their bedsteads: their dishevelled figures, mixed up with the shadows, looked broader, taller, and seemed to be growing bigger and bigger; on the furthest bedstead in the corner, where it was darkest, there sat the peasant moving his head and his hand.

Pashka, without noticing the doors, rushed into the smallpox ward, from there into the corridor, from the corridor he flew into a big room where monsters, with long hair and the faces of old women, were lying and sitting on the beds. Running through the women's wing he found himself again in the corridor, saw the banisters of the staircase he knew already, and ran downstairs. There he recognised the waiting-room in which he had sat that morning, and began looking for the door into the open air.

The latch creaked, there was a whiff of cold wind, and Pashka, stumbling, ran out into the yard. He had only one thought – to run, to run! He did not know the way, but felt convinced that if he ran he would be sure to find himself at home with his mother. The sky was overcast, but there was a moon behind the clouds. Pashka ran from the steps straight forward, went round the barn and stumbled into some thick bushes; after stopping for a minute and thinking, he dashed back again to the hospital, ran round it, and stopped again undecided; behind the hospital there were white crosses.

'Ma-a-mka!' he cried, and dashed back.

Running by the dark sinister buildings, he saw one lighted window.

The bright red patch looked dreadful in the darkness, but Pashka, frantic with terror, not knowing where to run, turned towards it. Beside the window was a porch with steps, and a front door with a white board on it; Pashka ran up the steps, looked in at the window, and was at once possessed by intense overwhelming joy. Through the window he saw the merry affable doctor sitting at the table reading a book. Laughing with happiness, Pashka stretched out his hands to the person he knew and tried to call out, but some unseen force choked him and struck at his legs; he staggered and fell down on the steps unconscious.

When he came to himself it was daylight, and a voice he knew very well, that had promised him a fair, finches, and a fox, was saying beside him:

'Well, you are an idiot, Pashka! Aren't you an idiot? You ought to be beaten, but there's no one to do it.'

Boys

'Volodya's come!' someone shouted in the yard.

'Master Volodya's here!' bawled Natalya the cook, running into the dining-room. 'Oh, my goodness!'

The whole Korolyov family, who had been expecting their Volodya from hour to hour, rushed to the windows. At the front door stood a wide sledge, with three white horses in a cloud of steam. The sledge was empty, for Volodya was already in the hall, untying his hood with red and chilly fingers. His school overcoat, his cap, his snowboots, and the hair on his temples were all white with frost, and his whole figure from head to foot diffused such a pleasant, fresh smell of the snow that the very sight of him made one want to shiver and say 'brrr!'

His mother and aunt ran to kiss and hug him. Natalya plumped down at his feet and began pulling off his snowboots, his sisters shrieked with delight, the doors creaked and banged, and Volodya's father, in his waistcoat and shirt-sleeves, ran out into the hall with scissors in his hand, and cried out in alarm:

'We were expecting you all yesterday? Did you come all right? Had a good journey? Mercy on us! you might let him say 'how do you do' to his father! I am his father after all!'

'Bow-wow!' barked the huge black dog, Milord, in a deep bass, tapping with his tail on the walls and furniture.

For two minutes there was nothing but a general hubbub of joy. After the first outburst of delight was over the Korolyovs noticed that there was, besides their Volodya, another small person in the hall, wrapped up in scarves and shawls and white with frost. He was standing perfectly still in a corner, in the shadow of a big fox-lined overcoat.

'Volodya darling, who is it?' asked his mother, in a whisper.

'Oh!' cried Volodya.' This is – let me introduce my friend Lentilov, a schoolfellow in the second class… I have brought him to stay with us.'

'Delighted to hear it! You are very welcome,' the father said cordially. 'Excuse me, I've been at work without my coat… Please come in! Natalya, help Mr. Lentilov off with his things. Mercy on us, do turn that dog out! He is unendurable!'

A few minutes later, Volodya and his friend Lentilov, somewhat dazed by their noisy welcome, and still red from the outside cold, were sitting down to tea. The winter sun, making its way through the snow and the frozen tracery on the window-panes, gleamed on the samovar, and plunged its pure rays in the tea-basin. The room was warm, and the boys felt as though the warmth and the frost were struggling together with a tingling sensation in their bodies.

'Well, Christmas will soon be here,' the father said in a pleasant sing-song voice, rolling a cigarette of dark reddish tobacco. 'It doesn't seem long since the summer, when mamma was crying at your going… and here you are back again… Time flies, my boy. Before you have time to cry out, old age is upon you. Mr. Lentilov, take some more, please help yourself! We don't stand on ceremony!'

Volodya's three sisters, Katya, Sonya, and Masha (the eldest was eleven), sat at the table and never took their eyes off the newcomer.

Lentilov was of the same height and age as Volodya, but not as round-faced and fair-skinned. He was thin, dark, and freckled; his hair stood up like a brush, his eyes were small, and his lips were thick. He was, in fact, distinctly ugly, and if he had not been wearing the school uniform, he might have been taken for the son of a cook. He seemed morose, did not speak, and never once smiled. The little girls, staring at him, immediately came to the conclusion that he must be a very clever and learned person. He seemed to be thinking about something all the time, and was so absorbed in his own thoughts, that, whenever he was spoken to, he started, threw his head back, and asked to have the question repeated.

The little girls noticed that Volodya, who had always been so merry and talkative, also said very little, did not smile at all, and hardly seemed to be glad to be home. All the time they were at tea he only once addressed his sisters, and then he said something so strange. He pointed to the samovar and said:

'In California they don't drink tea, but gin.'

He, too, seemed absorbed in his own thoughts, and, to judge by the looks that passed between him and his friend Lentilov, their thoughts were the same.

After tea, they all went into the nursery. The girls and their father took up the work that had been interrupted by the arrival of the boys. They were making flowers and frills for the Christmas tree out of paper of different colours. It was an attractive and noisy occupation. Every fresh flower was greeted by the little girls with shrieks of delight, even of awe, as though the flower had dropped straight from heaven; their father was in ecstasies too, and every now and then he threw the scissors on the floor, in vexation at their bluntness. Their mother kept running into the nursery with an anxious face, asking:

'Who has taken my scissors? Ivan Nikolaitch, have you taken my scissors again?'

'Mercy on us! I'm not even allowed a pair of scissors!' their father would respond in a lachrymose voice, and, flinging himself back in his chair, he would pretend to be a deeply injured man; but a minute later, he would be in ecstasies again.

On his former holidays Volodya, too, had taken part in the preparations for the Christmas tree, or had been running in the yard to look at the snow mountain that the watchman and the shepherd were building. But this time Volodya and Lentilov took no notice whatever of the coloured paper, and did not once go into the stable. They sat in the window and began whispering to one another; then they opened an atlas and looked carefully at a map.

First to Perm…' Lentilov said, in an undertone, 'from there to Tiumen, then Tomsk… then… then… Kamchatka. There the Samoyedes take one over Behring's Straits in boats… And then we are in America… There are lots of furry animals there…'

'And California?' asked Volodya.

'California is lower down… We've only to get to America and California is not far off… And one can get a living by hunting and plunder.'

All day long Lentilov avoided the little girls, and seemed to look at them with suspicion. In the evening he happened to be left alone with them for five minutes or so. It was awkward to be silent.

He cleared his throat morosely, rubbed his left hand against his right, looked sullenly at Katya and asked:

'Have you read Mayne Reid?'

'No, I haven't… I say, can you skate?'

Absorbed in his own reflections, Lentilov made no reply to this question; he simply puffed out his cheeks, and gave a long sigh as though he were very hot. He looked up at Katya once more and said:

'When a herd of bisons stampedes across the prairie the earth trembles, and the frightened mustangs kick and neigh.'

He smiled impressively and added:

'And the Indians attack the trains, too. But worst of all are the mosquitoes and the termites.'

'Why, what's that?'

'They're something like ants, but with wings. They bite fearfully. Do you know who I am?'

'Mr. Lentilov.'

'No, I am Montehomo, the Hawk's Claw, Chief of the Ever Victorious.'

Masha, the youngest, looked at him, then into the darkness out of window and said, wondering:

'And we had lentils for supper yesterday.'

Lentilov's incomprehensible utterances, and the way he was always whispering with Volodya, and the way Volodya seemed now to be always thinking about something instead of playing… all this was strange and mysterious. And the two elder girls, Katya and Sonya, began to keep a sharp look-out on the boys. At night, when the boys had gone to bed, the girls crept to their bedroom door, and listened to what they were saying. Ah, what they discovered! The boys were planning to run away to America to dig for gold: they had everything ready for the journey, a pistol, two knives, biscuits, a burning glass to serve instead of matches, a compass, and four roubles in cash. They learned that the boys would have to walk some thousands of miles, and would have to fight tigers and savages on the road: then they would get gold and ivory, slay their enemies, become pirates, drink gin, and finally marry beautiful maidens, and make a plantation.

The boys interrupted each other in their excitement. Throughout the conversation, Lentilov called himself 'Montehomo, the Hawk's Claw', and Volodya was 'my pale-face brother'!

'Mind you don't tell mamma,' said Katya, as they went back to bed. 'Volodya will bring us gold and ivory from America, but if you tell mamma he won't be allowed to go.'

The day before Christmas Eve, Lentilov spent the whole day poring over the map of Asia and making notes, while Volodya, with a languid and swollen face that looked as though it had been stung by a bee, walked about the rooms and ate nothing. And once he stood still before the holy image in the nursery, crossed himself, and said:

'Lord, forgive me a sinner; Lord, have pity on my poor unhappy mamma!'

In the evening he burst out crying. On saying goodnight he gave his father a long hug, and then hugged his mother and sisters. Katya and Sonya knew what was the matter, but little Masha was puzzled, completely puzzled. Every time she looked at Lentilov she grew thoughtful and said with a sigh:

'When Lent comes, nurse says we shall have to eat peas and lentils.'

Early in the morning of Christmas Eve, Katya and Sonya slipped quietly out of bed, and went to find out how the boys meant to run away to America. They crept to their door.

'Then you don't mean to go?' Lentilov was saying angrily. 'Speak out: aren't you going?'

'Oh dear,' Volodya wept softly. 'How can I go? I feel so unhappy about mamma.'

'My pale-face brother, I pray you, let us set off. You declared you were going, you egged me on, and now the time comes, you funk it!'

'I… I… I'm not funking it, but I… I… I'm sorry for mamma.'

'Say once and for all, are you going or are you not?'

'I am going, only… wait a little… I want to be at home a little.'

'In that case I will go by myself,' Lentilov declared. 'I can get on without you. And you wanted to hunt tigers and fight! Since that's how it is, give me back my cartridges!'

At this Volodya cried so bitterly that his sisters could not help crying too. Silence followed.

'So you are not coming?' Lentilov began again.

'I… I… I am coming!'

'Well, put on your things, then.'

And Lentilov tried to cheer Volodya up by singing the praises of America, growling like a tiger, pretending to be a steamer, scolding him, and promising to give him all the ivory and lions' and tigers' skins.

And this thin, dark boy, with his freckles and his bristling shock of hair, impressed the little girls as an extraordinary remarkable person. He was a hero, a determined character, who knew no fear, and he growled so ferociously, that, standing at the door, they really might imagine there was a tiger or lion inside. When the little girls went back to their room and dressed, Katya's eyes were full of tears, and she said:

'Oh, I feel so frightened!'

Everything was as usual till two o'clock, when they sat down to dinner. Then it appeared that the boys were not in the house. They sent to the servants' quarters, to the stables, to the bailiff's cottage. They were not to be found. They sent into the village – they were not there.

At tea, too, the boys were still absent, and by supper-time Volodya's mother was dreadfully uneasy, and even shed tears.

Late in the evening they sent again to the village, they searched everywhere, and walked along the river bank with lanterns. Heavens! what a fuss there was!

Next day the police officer came, and a paper of some sort was written out in the dining-room. Their mother cried…

All of a sudden a sledge stopped at the door, with three white horses in a cloud of steam.

'Volodya's come,' someone shouted in the yard.

'Master Volodya's here!' bawled Natalya, running into the dining-room. And Milord barked his deep bass, 'bow-wow.'

It seemed that the boys had been stopped in the Arcade, where they had gone from shop to shop asking where they could get gunpowder.

Volodya burst into sobs as soon as he came into the hall, and flung himself on his mother's neck. The little girls, trembling, wondered with terror what would happen next. They saw their father take Volodya and Lentilov into his study, and there he talked to them a long while.

'Is this a proper thing to do?' their father said to them. 'I only pray they won't hear of it at school, you would both be expelled. You ought to be ashamed, Mr. Lentilov, really. It's not at all the thing to do! You began it, and I hope you will be punished by your parents. How could you? Where did you spend the night?'

'At the station,' Lentilov answered proudly.

Then Volodya went to bed, and had a compress, steeped in vinegar, on his forehead.

A telegram was sent off, and next day a lady, Lentilov's mother, made her appearance and bore off her son.

Lentilov looked morose and haughty to the end, and he did not utter a single word at taking leave of the little girls. But he took Katya's book and wrote in it as a souvenir: 'Montehomo, the Hawk's Claw, Chief of the Ever Victorious.'

Sleepy

Night. Varka, the little nurse, a girl of thirteen, is rocking the cradle in which the baby is lying, and humming hardly audibly:

> 'Hush–a–bye, my baby wee,
> While I sing a song for thee.'

A little green lamp is burning before the ikon; there is a string stretched from one end of the room to the other, on which baby-clothes and a pair of big black trousers are hanging. There is a big patch of green on the ceiling from the ikon lamp, and the baby-clothes and the trousers throw long shadows on the stove, on the cradle, and on Varka… When the lamp begins to flicker, the green patch and the shadows come to life, and are set in motion, as though by the wind. It is stuffy. There is a smell of cabbage soup, and of the inside of a boot-shop.

The baby's crying. For a long while he has been hoarse and exhausted with crying; but he still goes on screaming, and there is no knowing when he will stop. And Varka is sleepy. Her eyes are glued together, her head droops, her neck aches. She cannot move her eyelids or her lips, and she feels as though her face is dried and wooden, as though her head has become as small as the head of a pin.

'Hush-a-bye, my baby wee,' she hums, 'while I cook the groats for thee…'

A cricket is churring in the stove. Through the door in the next room the master and the apprentice Afanasy are snoring… The cradle creaks plaintively, Varka murmurs – and it all blends into that soothing music of the night to which it is so sweet to listen, when one is lying in bed. Now that music is merely irritating and oppressive, because it goads her to sleep, and she must not sleep; if Varka – God forbid! – should fall asleep, her master and mistress would beat her.

The lamp flickers. The patch of green and the shadows are set in motion, forcing themselves on Varka's fixed, half-open eyes, and in her half slumbering brain are fashioned into misty visions. She sees dark clouds chasing one another over the sky, and screaming like the baby. But then the wind blows, the clouds are gone, and Varka sees a broad high road covered with liquid mud; along the high road stretch files of wagons, while people with wallets on their backs are trudging along and shadows flit backwards and forwards; on both sides she can see forests through the cold harsh mist. All at once the people with their wallets and their shadows fall on the ground in the liquid mud. 'What is that for?' Varka asks. 'To sleep, to sleep!' they answer her. And they fall sound asleep, and sleep sweetly, while crows and magpies sit on the telegraph wires, scream like the baby, and try to wake them.

'Hush-a-bye, my baby wee, and I will sing a song to thee,' murmurs Varka, and now she sees herself in a dark stuffy hut.

Her dead father, Yefim Stepanov, is tossing from side to side on the floor. She does not see him, but she hears him moaning and rolling on the floor from pain. 'His guts have burst,' as he says; the pain is so violent that he cannot utter a single word, and can only draw in his breath and clack his teeth like the rattling of a drum:

'Boo–boo–boo–boo…'

Her mother, Pelageya, has run to the master's house to say that Yefim is dying. She has been gone a long time, and ought to be back.

Varka lies awake on the stove, and hears her father's 'boo–boo–boo.'
And then she hears someone has driven up to the hut. It is a young
doctor from the town, who has been sent from the big house where
he is staying on a visit. The doctor comes into the hut; he cannot be
seen in the darkness, but he can be heard coughing and rattling the
door.

'Light a candle,' he says.

'Boo–boo–boo,' answers Yefim.

Pelageya rushes to the stove and begins looking for the broken
pot with the matches. A minute passes in silence. The doctor, feeling
in his pocket, lights a match.

'In a minute, sir, in a minute,' says Pelageya. She rushes out of the
hut, and soon afterwards comes back with a bit of candle.

Yefim's cheeks are rosy and his eyes are shining, and there is a
peculiar keenness in his glance, as though he were seeing right through
the hut and the doctor.

'Come, what is it? What are you thinking about?' says the doctor,
bending down to him. 'Aha! have you had this long?'

'What? Dying, your honour, my hour has come… I am not to stay
among the living.'

'Don't talk nonsense! We will cure you!'

'That's as you please, your honour, we humbly thank you, only
we understand… Since death has come, there it is.'

The doctor spends a quarter of an hour over Yefim, then he gets
up and says:

'I can do nothing. You must go into the hospital, there they will
operate on you. Go at once… You must go! It's rather late, they will
all be asleep in the hospital, but that doesn't matter, I will give you a
note. Do you hear?'

'Kind sir, but what can he go in?' says Pelageya. 'We have no horse.'

'Never mind. I'll ask your master, he'll let you have a horse.'

The doctor goes away, the candle goes out, and again there is the
sound of 'boo–boo–boo.' Half an hour later someone drives up to the
hut. A cart has been sent to take Yefim to the hospital. He gets ready
and goes…

But now it is a clear bright morning. Pelageya is not at home; she has gone to the hospital to find what is being done to Yefim. Somewhere there is a baby crying, and Varka hears someone singing with her own voice:

'Hush-a-bye, my baby wee, I will sing a song to thee.'

Pelageya comes back; she crosses herself and whispers:

'They put him to rights in the night, but towards morning he gave up his soul to God... The Kingdom of Heaven be his and peace everlasting... They say he was taken too late... He ought to have gone sooner...'

Varka goes out into the road and cries there, but all at once someone hits her on the back of her head so hard that her forehead knocks against a birch tree. She raises her eyes, and sees facing her, her master, the shoemaker.

'What are you about, you scabby slut?' he says. 'The child is crying, and you are asleep!'

He gives her a sharp slap behind the ear, and she shakes her head, rocks the cradle, and murmurs her song. The green patch and the shadows from the trousers and the baby-clothes move up and down, nod to her, and soon take possession of her brain again. Again she sees the high road covered with liquid mud. The people with wallets on their backs and the shadows have lain down and are fast asleep. Looking at them, Varka has a passionate longing for sleep; she would lie down with enjoyment, but her mother Pelageya is walking beside her, hurrying her on. They are hastening together to the town to find situations.

'Give alms, for Christ's sake!' her mother begs of the people they meet. 'Show us the Divine Mercy, kind-hearted gentlefolk!'

'Give the baby here!' a familiar voice answers. 'Give the baby here!' the same voice repeats, this time harshly and angrily. 'Are you asleep, you wretched girl?'

Varka jumps up, and looking round grasps what is the matter: there is no high road, no Pelageya, no people meeting them, there is only her mistress, who has come to feed the baby, and is standing in the middle of the room. While the stout, broad-shouldered woman nurses the child and soothes it, Varka stands looking at her and waiting till she has done. And outside the windows the air is already turning blue, the shadows and the green patch on the ceiling are visibly growing pale, it will soon be morning.

'Take him,' says her mistress, buttoning up her chemise over her bosom; 'he is crying. He must be bewitched.'

Varka takes the baby, puts him in the cradle and begins rocking it again. The green patch and the shadows gradually disappear, and now there is nothing to force itself on her eyes and cloud her brain. But she is as sleepy as before, fearfully sleepy! Varka lays her head on the edge of the cradle, and rocks her whole body to overcome her sleepiness, but yet her eyes are glued together, and her head is heavy.

'Varka, heat the stove!' she hears the master's voice through the door.

So it is time to get up and set to work. Varka leaves the cradle, and runs to the shed for firewood. She is glad. When one moves and runs about, one is not so sleepy as when one is sitting down. She brings the wood, heats the stove, and feels that her wooden face is getting supple again, and that her thoughts are growing clearer.

'Varka, set the samovar!' shouts her mistress.

Varka splits a piece of wood, but has scarcely time to light the splinters and put them in the samovar, when she hears a fresh order:

'Varka, clean the master's goloshes!'

She sits down on the floor, cleans the goloshes, and thinks how nice it would be to put her head into a big deep golosh, and have a little nap in it… And all at once the golosh grows, swells, fills up the whole room. Varka drops the brush, but at once shakes her head, opens her eyes wide, and tries to look at things so that they may not grow big and move before her eyes.

'Varka, wash the steps outside; I am ashamed for the customers to see them!'

Varka washes the steps, sweeps and dusts the rooms, then heats another stove and runs to the shop. There is a great deal of work: she hasn't one minute free.

But nothing is so hard as standing in the same place at the kitchen table peeling potatoes. Her head droops over the table, the potatoes dance before her eyes, the knife tumbles out of her hand while her fat, angry mistress is moving about near her with her sleeves tucked up, talking so loud that it makes a ringing in Varka's ears. It is agonising, too, to wait at dinner, to wash, to sew, there are minutes when she longs to flop on to the floor regardless of everything, and to sleep.

The day passes. Seeing the windows getting dark, Varka presses her temples that feel as though they were made of wood, and smiles, though she does not know why. The dusk of evening caresses her eyes that will hardly keep open, and promises her sound sleep soon. In the evening visitors come.

'Varka, set the samovar!' shouts her mistress. The samovar is a little one, and before the visitors have drunk all the tea they want, she has to heat it five times. After tea Varka stands for a whole hour on the same spot, looking at the visitors, and waiting for orders.

'Varka, run and buy three bottles of beer!'

She starts off, and tries to run as quickly as she can, to drive away sleep.

'Varka, fetch some vodka! Varka, where's the corkscrew? Varka, clean a herring!'

But now, at last, the visitors have gone; the lights are put out, the master and mistress go to bed.

'Varka, rock the baby!' she hears the last order.

The cricket churrs in the stove; the green patch on the ceiling and the shadows from the trousers and the baby-clothes force themselves on Varka's half-opened eyes again, wink at her and cloud her mind.

'Hush-a-bye, my baby wee,' she murmurs, 'and I will sing a song to thee.'

And the baby screams, and is worn out with screaming. Again Varka sees the muddy high road, the people with wallets, her mother Pelageya, her father Yefim. She understands everything, she recognises everyone, but through her half sleep she cannot understand the force which binds her, hand and foot, weighs upon her, and prevents her from living. She looks round, searches for that force that she may escape from it, but she cannot find it. At last, tired to death, she does her very utmost, strains her eyes, looks up at the flickering green patch, and listening to the screaming, finds the foe who will not let her live.

That foe is the baby.

She laughs. It seems strange to her that she has failed to grasp such a simple thing before. The green patch, the shadows, and the cricket seem to laugh and wonder too.

The hallucination takes possession of Varka. She gets up from her stool, and with a broad smile on her face and wide unblinking eyes, she walks up and down the room. She feels pleased and tickled at the thought that she will be rid directly of the baby that binds her hand and foot… Kill the baby and then sleep, sleep, sleep…

Laughing and winking and shaking her fingers at the green patch, Varka steals up to the cradle and bends over the baby. When she has strangled him, she quickly lies down on the floor, laughs with delight that she can sleep, and in a minute is sleeping as sound as the dead.

Rothschild's Fiddle

The town was a little one, worse than a village, and it was inhabited by scarcely any but old people who died with an infrequency that was really annoying. In the hospital and in the prison fortress very few coffins were needed. In fact business was bad. If Yakov Ivanov had been an undertaker in the chief town of the province he would certainly have had a house of his own, and people would have addressed him as Yakov Matveyitch; here in this wretched little town people called him simply Yakov; his nickname in the street was for some reason Bronze, and he lived in a poor way like a humble peasant, in a little old hut in which there was only one room, and in this room he and Marfa, the stove, a double bed, the coffins, his bench, and all their belongings were crowded together.

Yakov made good, solid coffins. For peasants and working people he made them to fit himself, and this was never unsuccessful, for there were none taller and stronger than he, even in the prison, though he was seventy. For gentry and for women he made them to measure, and used an iron foot-rule for the purpose. He was very unwilling to take orders for children's coffins, and made them straight off without measurements, contemptuously, and when he was paid for the work he always said:

'I must confess I don't like trumpery jobs.'

Apart from his trade, playing the fiddle brought him in a small income.

The Jews' orchestra conducted by Moisey Ilyitch Shahkes, the tinsmith, who took more than half their receipts for himself, played as a rule at weddings in the town. As Yakov played very well on the fiddle, especially Russian songs, Shahkes sometimes invited him to join the orchestra at a fee of half a rouble a day, in addition to tips from the visitors. When Bronze sat in the orchestra first of all his face became crimson and perspiring; it was hot, there was a suffocating smell of garlic, the fiddle squeaked, the double bass wheezed close to his right ear, while the flute wailed at his left, played by a gaunt, red-haired Jew who had a perfect network of red and blue veins all over his face, and who bore the name of the famous millionaire Rothschild. And this accursed Jew contrived to play even the liveliest things plaintively. For no apparent reason Yakov little by little became possessed by hatred and contempt for the Jews, and especially for Rothschild; he began to pick quarrels with him, rail at him in unseemly language and once even tried to strike him, and Rothschild was offended and said, looking at him ferociously:

'If it were not that I respect you for your talent, I would have sent you flying out of the window.'

Then he began to weep. And because of this Yakov was not often asked to play in the orchestra; he was only sent for in case of extreme necessity in the absence of one of the Jews.

Yakov was never in a good temper, as he was continually having to put up with terrible losses. For instance, it was a sin to work on Sundays or Saints' days, and Monday was an unlucky day, so that in the course of the year there were some two hundred days on which, whether he liked it or not, he had to sit with his hands folded. And only think, what a loss that meant. If anyone in the town had a wedding without music, or if Shahkes did not send for Yakov, that was a loss, too. The superintendent of the prison was ill for two years and was wasting away, and Yakov was impatiently waiting for him to die, but the superintendent went away to the chief town of the province to be doctored, and there took and died. There's a loss for you, ten roubles at least, as there would have been an expensive coffin to make, lined with brocade. The thought of his losses haunted Yakov, especially at night; he laid his fiddle on the bed beside him, and when all sorts of nonsensical ideas came into his mind he touched a string; the fiddle gave out a sound in the darkness, and he felt better.

On the sixth of May of the previous year Marfa had suddenly been taken ill. The old woman's breathing was laboured, she drank a great deal of water, and she staggered as she walked, yet she lighted the stove in the morning and even went herself to get water. Towards evening she lay down. Yakov played his fiddle all day; when it was quite dark he took the book in which he used every day to put down his losses, and, feeling dull, he began adding up the total for the year. It came to more than a thousand roubles. This so agitated him that he flung the reckoning beads down, and trampled them under his feet. Then he picked up the reckoning beads, and again spent a long time clicking with them and heaving deep, strained sighs. His face was crimson and wet with perspiration. He thought that if he had put that lost thousand roubles in the bank, the interest for a year would have been at least forty roubles, so that forty roubles was a loss too. In fact, wherever one turned there were losses and nothing else.

'Yakov!' Marfa called unexpectedly. 'I am dying.'

He looked round at his wife. Her face was rosy with fever, unusually bright and joyful-looking. Bronze, accustomed to seeing her face always pale, timid, and unhappy-looking, was bewildered. It looked as if she really were dying and were glad that she was going away for ever from that hut, from the coffins, and from Yakov… And she gazed at the ceiling and moved her lips, and her expression was one of happiness, as though she saw death as her deliverer and were whispering with him.

It was daybreak; from the windows one could see the flush of dawn. Looking at the old woman, Yakov for some reason reflected that he had not once in his life been affectionate to her, had had no feeling for her, had never once thought to buy her a kerchief, or to bring her home some dainty from a wedding, but had done nothing but shout at her, scold her for his losses, shake his fists at her; it is true he had never actually beaten her, but he had frightened her, and at such times she had always been numb with terror. Why, he had forbidden her to drink tea because they spent too much without that, and she drank only hot water. And he understood why she had such a strange, joyful face now, and he was overcome with dread.

As soon as it was morning he borrowed a horse from a neighbour and took Marfa to the hospital. There were not many patients there, and so he had not long to wait, only three hours. To his great satisfaction the patients were not being received by the doctor, who was himself ill, but by the assistant, Maxim Nikolaitch, an old man of whom everyone in the town used to say that, though he drank and was quarrelsome, he knew more than the doctor.

'I wish you good-day,' said Yakov, leading his old woman into the consulting room. 'You must excuse us, Maxim Nikolaitch, we are always troubling you with our trumpery affairs. Here you see my better half is ailing, the partner of my life, as they say, excuse the expression...'

Knitting his grizzled brows and stroking his whiskers the assistant began to examine the old woman, and she sat on a stool, a wasted, bent figure with a sharp nose and open mouth, looking like a bird that wants to drink.

'H——m... Ah!...' the assistant said slowly, and he heaved a sigh. 'Influenza and possibly fever. There's typhus in the town now. Well, the old woman has lived her life, thank God... How old is she?'

'She'll be seventy in another year, Maxim Nikolaitch.'

'Well, the old woman has lived her life, it's time to say goodbye.'

'You are quite right in what you say, of course, Maxim Nikolaitch,' said Yakov, smiling from politeness, 'and we thank you feelingly for your kindness, but allow me to say every insect wants to live.'

'To be sure,' said the assistant, in a tone which suggested that it depended upon him whether the woman lived or died. 'Well, then, my good fellow, put a cold compress on her head, and give her these powders twice a day, and so goodbye. Bonjour.'

From the expression of his face Yakov saw that it was a bad case, and that no sort of powders would be any help; it was clear to him that Marfa would die very soon, if not today, tomorrow. He nudged the assistant's elbow, winked at him, and said in a low voice:

'If you would just cup her, Maxim Nikolaitch.'

'I have no time, I have no time, my good fellow. Take your old woman and go in God's name. Goodbye.'

'Be so gracious,' Yakov besought him. 'You know yourself that if, let us say, it were her stomach or her inside that were bad, then powders or drops, but you see she had got a chill! In a chill the first thing is to let blood, Maxim Nikolaitch.'

But the assistant had already sent for the next patient, and a peasant woman came into the consulting room with a boy.

'Go along! go along,' he said to Yakov, frowning. 'It's no use to —'

'In that case put on leeches, anyway! Make us pray for you for ever.'

The assistant flew into a rage and shouted:

'You speak to me again! You blockhead…'

Yakov flew into a rage too, and he turned crimson all over, but he did not utter a word. He took Marfa on his arm and led her out of the room. Only when they were sitting in the cart he looked morosely and ironically at the hospital, and said:

'A nice set of artists they have settled here! No fear, but he would have cupped a rich man, but even a leech he grudges to the poor. The Herods!'

When they got home and went into the hut, Marfa stood for ten minutes holding on to the stove. It seemed to her that if she were to lie down Yakov would talk to her about his losses, and scold her for lying down and not wanting to work. Yakov looked at her drearily and thought that tomorrow was St. John the Divine's, and next day St. Nikolay the Wonder-worker's, and the day after that was Sunday, and then Monday, an unlucky day. For four days he would not be able to work, and most likely Marfa would die on one of those days; so he would have to make the coffin today. He picked up his iron rule, went up to the old woman and took her measure. Then she lay down, and he crossed himself and began making the coffin.

When the coffin was finished Bronze put on his spectacles and wrote in his book: 'Marfa Ivanov's coffin, two roubles, forty kopecks.'

And he heaved a sigh. The old woman lay all the time silent with her eyes closed. But in the evening, when it got dark, she suddenly called the old man.

'Do you remember, Yakov,' she asked, looking at him joyfully. 'Do you remember fifty years ago God gave us a little baby with flaxen hair? We used always to be sitting by the river then, singing songs… under the willows,' and laughing bitterly, she added: 'The baby girl died.'

Yakov racked his memory, but could not remember the baby or the willows.

'It's your fancy,' he said.

The priest arrived; he administered the sacrament and extreme unction. Then Marfa began muttering something unintelligible, and towards morning she died. Old women, neighbours, washed her, dressed her, and laid her in the coffin. To avoid paying the sacristan, Yakov read the psalms over the body himself, and they got nothing out of him for the grave, as the grave-digger was a crony of his. Four peasants carried the coffin to the graveyard, not for money, but from respect. The coffin was followed by old women, beggars, and a couple of crazy saints, and the people who met it crossed themselves piously… And Yakov was very much pleased that it was so creditable, so decorous, and so cheap, and no offence to anyone. As he took his last leave of Marfa he touched the coffin and thought: 'A good piece of work!'

But as he was going back from the cemetery he was overcome by acute depression. He didn't feel quite well: his breathing was laboured and feverish, his legs felt weak, and he had a craving for drink. And thoughts of all sorts forced themselves on his mind. He remembered again that all his life he had never felt for Marfa, had never been affectionate to her. The fifty-two years they had lived in the same hut had dragged on a long, long time, but it had somehow happened that in all that time he had never once thought of her, had paid no attention to her, as though she had been a cat or a dog. And yet, every day, she had lighted the stove had cooked and baked, had gone for the water, had chopped the wood, had slept with him in the same bed, and when he came home drunk from the weddings always reverently hung his fiddle on the wall and put him to bed, and all this in silence, with a timid, anxious expression.

Rothschild, smiling and bowing, came to meet Yakov.

'I was looking for you, uncle,' he said. 'Moisey Ilyitch sends you his greetings and bids you come to him at once.'

Yakov felt in no mood for this. He wanted to cry.

'Leave me alone,' he said, and walked on.

'How can you,' Rothschild said, fluttered, running on in front. 'Moisey Ilyitch will be offended! He bade you come at once!'

Yakov was revolted at the Jew's gasping for breath and blinking, and having so many red freckles on his face. And it was disgusting to look at his green coat with black patches on it, and all his fragile, refined figure.

'Why are you pestering me, garlic?' shouted Yakov. 'Don't persist!'

The Jew got angry and shouted too:

'Not so noisy, please, or I'll send you flying over the fence!'

'Get out of my sight!' roared Yakov, and rushed at him with his fists. 'One can't live for you scabby Jews!'

Rothschild, half dead with terror, crouched down and waved his hands over his head, as though to ward off a blow; then he leapt up and ran away as fast as his legs could carry him: as he ran he gave little skips and kept clasping his hands, and Yakov could see how his long thin spine wriggled. Some boys, delighted at the incident, ran after him shouting 'Jew! Jew!' Some dogs joined in the chase barking. Someone burst into a roar of laughter, then gave a whistle; the dogs barked with even more noise and unanimity. Then a dog must have bitten Rothschild, as a desperate, sickly scream was heard.

Yakov went for a walk on the grazing ground, then wandered on at random in the outskirts of the town, while the street boys shouted:

'Here's Bronze! Here's Bronze!'

He came to the river, where the curlews floated in the air uttering shrill cries and the ducks quacked. The sun was blazing hot, and there was a glitter from the water, so that it hurt the eyes to look at it. Yakov walked by a path along the bank and saw a plump, rosy-cheeked lady come out of the bathing-shed, and thought about her: 'Ugh! you otter!'

Not far from the bathing-shed boys were catching crayfish with bits of meat; seeing him, they began shouting spitefully, 'Bronze! Bronze!' And then he saw an old spreading willow-tree with a big hollow in it, and a crow's nest on it… And suddenly there rose up vividly in Yakov's memory a baby with flaxen hair, and the willow-tree Marfa had spoken of. Why, that is it, the same willow-tree – green, still, and sorrowful… How old it has grown, poor thing!

He sat down under it and began to recall the past. On the other bank, where now there was the water meadow, in those days there stood a big birchwood, and yonder on the bare hillside that could be seen on the horizon an old, old pine forest used to be a bluish patch in the distance. Big boats used to sail on the river. But now it was all smooth and unruffled, and on the other bank there stood now only one birch-tree, youthful and slender like a young lady, and there was nothing on the river but ducks and geese, and it didn't look as though there had ever been boats on it. It seemed as though even the geese were fewer than of old. Yakov shut his eyes, and in his imagination huge flocks of white geese soared, meeting one another.

He wondered how it had happened that for the last forty or fifty years of his life he had never once been to the river, or if he had been by it he had not paid attention to it. Why, it was a decent sized river, not a trumpery one; he might have gone in for fishing and sold the fish to merchants, officials, and the bar-keeper at the station, and then have put money in the bank; he might have sailed in a boat from one house to another, playing the fiddle, and people of all classes would have paid to hear him; he might have tried getting big boats afloat again – that would be better than making coffins; he might have bred geese, killed them and sent them in the winter to Moscow. Why, the feathers alone would very likely mount up to ten roubles in the year. But he had wasted his time, he had done nothing of this. What losses! Ah! What losses! And if he had gone in for all those things at once – catching fish and playing the fiddle, and running boats and killing geese – what a fortune he would have made! But nothing of this had happened, even in his dreams; life had passed uselessly without any pleasure, had been wasted for nothing, not even a pinch of snuff; there was nothing left in front, and if one looked back – there was nothing there but losses, and such terrible ones, it made one cold all over. And why was it a man could not live so as to avoid these losses and misfortunes? One wondered why they had cut down the birch copse and the pine forest. Why was he walking with no reason on the grazing ground? Why do people always do what isn't needful? Why had Yakov all his life scolded, bellowed, shaken his fists, ill-treated his wife, and, one might ask, what necessity was there for him to frighten and insult the Jew that day? Why did people in general hinder each other from living? What losses were due to it! what terrible losses! If it were not for hatred and malice people would get immense benefit from one another.

In the evening and the night he had visions of the baby, of the willow, of fish, of slaughtered geese, and Marfa looking in profile like a bird that wants to drink, and the pale, pitiful face of Rothschild, and faces moved down from all sides and muttered of losses. He tossed from side to side, and got out of bed five times to play the fiddle.

In the morning he got up with an effort and went to the hospital. The same Maxim Nikolaitch told him to put a cold compress on his head, and gave him some powders, and from his tone and expression of face Yakov realized that it was a bad case and that no powders would be any use. As he went home afterwards, he reflected that death would be nothing but a benefit; he would not have to eat or drink, or pay taxes or offend people, and, as a man lies in his grave not for one year but for hundreds and thousands, if one reckoned it up the gain would be enormous. A man's life meant loss: death meant gain. This reflection was, of course, a just one, but yet it was bitter and mortifying; why was the order of the world so strange, that life, which is given to man only once, passes away without benefit?

He was not sorry to die, but at home, as soon as he saw his fiddle, it sent a pang to his heart and he felt sorry. He could not take the fiddle with him to the grave, and now it would be left forlorn, and the same thing would happen to it as to the birch copse and the pine forest. Everything in this world was wasted and would be wasted! Yakov went out of the hut and sat in the doorway, pressing the fiddle to his bosom. Thinking of his wasted, profitless life, he began to play, he did not know what, but it was plaintive and touching, and tears trickled down his cheeks. And the harder he thought, the more mournfully the fiddle wailed.

The latch clicked once and again, and Rothschild appeared at the gate. He walked across half the yard boldly, but seeing Yakov he stopped short, and seemed to shrink together, and probably from terror, began making signs with his hands as though he wanted to show on his fingers what o'clock it was.

'Come along, it's all right,' said Yakov in a friendly tone, and he beckoned him to come up. 'Come along!'

Looking at him mistrustfully and apprehensively, Rothschild began to advance, and stopped seven feet off.

'Be so good as not to beat me,' he said, ducking. 'Moisey Ilyitch has sent me again. 'Don't be afraid,' he said; 'go to Yakov again and tell him,' he said, 'we can't get on without him.' There is a wedding on Wednesday… Ye-es! Mr. Shapovalov is marrying his daughter to a good man… And it will be a grand wedding, oo-oo!' added the Jew, screwing up one eye.

'I can't come,' said Yakov, breathing hard. 'I'm ill, brother.'

And he began playing again, and the tears gushed from his eyes on to the fiddle. Rothschild listened attentively, standing sideways to him and folding his arms on his chest. The scared and perplexed expression on his face, little by little, changed to a look of woe and suffering; he rolled his eyes as though he were experiencing an agonizing ecstasy, and articulated, 'Vachhh!' and tears slowly ran down his cheeks and trickled on his greenish coat.

And Yakov lay in bed all the rest of the day grieving. In the evening, when the priest confessing him asked, Did he remember any special sin he had committed? straining his failing memory he thought again of Marfa's unhappy face, and the despairing shriek of the Jew when the dog bit him, and said, hardly audibly, 'Give the fiddle to Rothschild.'

'Very well,' answered the priest.

And now everyone in the town asks where Rothschild got such a fine fiddle. Did he buy it or steal it? Or perhaps it had come to him as a pledge. He gave up the flute long ago, and now plays nothing but the fiddle. As plaintive sounds flow now from his bow, as came once from his flute, but when he tries to repeat what Yakov played, sitting in the doorway, the effect is something so sad and sorrowful that his audience weep, and he himself rolls his eyes and articulates 'Vachhh!…' And this new air was so much liked in the town that the merchants and officials used to be continually sending for Rothschild and making him play it over and over again a dozen times.

The Head Gardener's Story

A sale of flowers was taking place in Count N.'s greenhouses. The purchasers were few in number – a landowner who was a neighbor of mine, a young timber-merchant, and myself. While the workmen were carrying out our magnificent purchases and packing them into the carts, we sat at the entry of the greenhouse and chatted about one thing and another. It is extremely pleasant to sit in a garden on a still April morning, listening to the birds, and watching the flowers brought out into the open air and basking in the sunshine.

The head-gardener, Mihail Karlovitch, a venerable old man with a full shaven face, wearing a fur waistcoat and no coat, superintended the packing of the plants himself, but at the same time he listened to our conversation in the hope of hearing something new. He was an intelligent, very good-hearted man, respected by everyone. He was for some reason looked upon by everyone as a German, though he was in reality on his father's side Swedish, on his mother's side Russian, and attended the Orthodox church. He knew Russian, Swedish, and German. He had read a good deal in those languages, and nothing one

127

could do gave him greater pleasure than lending him some new book or talking to him, for instance, about Ibsen.

He had his weaknesses, but they were innocent ones: he called himself the head gardener, though there were no under-gardeners; the expression of his face was unusually dignified and haughty; he could not endure to be contradicted, and liked to be listened to with respect and attention.

'That young fellow there I can recommend to you as an awful rascal,' said my neighbour, pointing to a labourer with a swarthy, gipsy face, who drove by with the water-barrel. 'Last week he was tried in the town for burglary and was acquitted; they pronounced him mentally deranged, and yet look at him, he is the picture of health. Scoundrels are very often acquitted nowadays in Russia on grounds of abnormality and aberration, yet these acquittals, these unmistakable proofs of an indulgent attitude to crime, lead to no good. They demoralize the masses, the sense of justice is blunted in all as they become accustomed to seeing vice unpunished, and you know in our age one may boldly say in the words of Shakespeare that in our evil and corrupt age virtue must ask forgiveness of vice.'

'That's very true,' the merchant assented. 'Owing to these frequent acquittals, murder and arson have become much more common. Ask the peasants.'

Mihail Karlovitch turned towards us and said:

'As far as I am concerned, gentlemen, I am always delighted to meet with these verdicts of not guilty. I am not afraid for morality and justice when they say 'Not guilty,' but on the contrary I feel pleased. Even when my conscience tells me the jury have made a mistake in acquitting the criminal, even then I am triumphant. Judge for yourselves, gentlemen; if the judges and the jury have more faith in *man* than in evidence, material proofs, and speeches for the prosecution, is not that faith *in man* in itself higher than any ordinary considerations? Such faith is only attainable by those few who understand and feel Christ.'

'A fine thought,' I said.

'But it's not a new one. I remember a very long time ago I heard a legend on that subject. A very charming legend,' said the gardener, and he smiled. 'I was told it by my grandmother, my father's mother, an excellent old lady. She told me it in Swedish, and it does not sound so fine, so classical, in Russian.'

But we begged him to tell it and not to be put off by the coarseness of the Russian language. Much gratified, he deliberately lighted his pipe, looked angrily at the labourers, and began:

'There settled in a certain little town a solitary, plain, elderly gentleman called Thomson or Wilson – but that does not matter; the surname is not the point. He followed an honourable profession: he was a doctor. He was always morose and unsociable, and only spoke when required by his profession. He never visited anyone, never extended his acquaintance beyond a silent bow, and lived as humbly as a hermit. The fact was, he was a learned man, and in those days learned men were not like other people. They spent their days and nights in contemplation, in reading and in healing disease, looked upon everything else as trivial, and had no time to waste a word. The inhabitants of the town understood this, and tried not to worry him with their visits and empty chatter. They were very glad that God had sent them at last a man who could heal diseases, and were proud that such a remarkable man was living in their town. 'He knows everything,' they said about him.

'But that was not enough. They ought to have also said, 'He loves everyone.' In the breast of that learned man there beat a wonderful angelic heart. Though the people of that town were strangers and not his own people, yet he loved them like children, and did not spare himself for them. He was himself ill with consumption, he had a cough, but when he was summoned to the sick he forgot his own illness he did not spare himself and, gasping for breath, climbed up the hills however high they might be. He disregarded the sultry heat and the cold, despised thirst and hunger. He would accept no money and strange to say, when one of his patients died, he would follow the coffin with the relations, weeping.

'And soon he became so necessary to the town that the inhabitants wondered how they could have got on before without the man. Their gratitude knew no bounds. Grown-up people and children, good and bad alike, honest men and cheats – all in fact, respected him and knew his value. In the little town and all the surrounding neighborhood there was no man who would allow himself to do anything disagreeable to him; indeed, they would never have dreamed of it. When he came out of his lodging, he never fastened the doors or windows, in complete confidence that there was no thief who could bring himself to do him wrong. He often had in the course of his medical duties to walk along the highroads, through the forests and mountains haunted by numbers of hungry vagrants; but he felt that he was in perfect security.

'One night he was returning from a patient when robbers fell upon him in the forest, but when they recognized him, they took off their hats respectfully and offered him something to eat. When he answered that he was not hungry, they gave him a warm wrap and accompanied him as far as the town, happy that fate had given them the chance in some small way to show their gratitude to the benevolent man. Well, to be sure, my grandmother told me that even the horses and the cows and the dogs knew him and expressed their joy when they met him.

'And this man who seemed by his sanctity to have guarded himself from every evil, to whom even brigands and frenzied men wished nothing but good, was one fine morning found murdered. Covered with blood, with his skull broken, he was lying in a ravine, and his pale face wore an expression of amazement. Yes, not horror but amazement was the emotion that had been fixed upon his face when he saw the murderer before him. You can imagine the grief that overwhelmed the inhabitants of the town and the surrounding districts. All were in despair, unable to believe their eyes, wondering who could have killed the man. The judges who conducted the inquiry and examined the doctor's body said: 'Here we have all the signs of a murder, but as there is not a man in the world capable of murdering our doctor, obviously it was not a case of murder, and the combination of evidence is due to simple chance. We must suppose that in the darkness he fell into the ravine of himself and was mortally injured.'

'The whole town agreed with this opinion. The doctor was buried, and nothing more was said about a violent death. The existence of a man who could have the baseness and wickedness to kill the doctor seemed incredible. There is a limit even to wickedness, isn't there?

'All at once, would you believe it, chance led them to discovering the murderer. A vagrant who had been many times convicted, notorious for his vicious life, was seen selling for drink a snuff-box and watch that had belonged to the doctor. When he was questioned he was confused, and answered with an obvious lie. A search was made, and in his bed was found a shirt with stains of blood on the sleeves, and a doctor's lancet set in gold. What more evidence was wanted? They put the criminal in prison. The inhabitants were indignant, and at the same time said:

'It's incredible! It can't be so! Take care that a mistake is not made; it does happen, you know, that evidence tells a false tale.'

'At his trial the murderer obstinately denied his guilt. Everything was against him, and to be convinced of his guilt was as easy as to believe that this earth is black; but the judges seem to have gone mad: they weighed every proof ten times, looked distrustfully at the witnesses, flushed crimson and sipped water… The trial began early in the morning and was only finished in the evening.

'Accused!' the chief judge said, addressing the murderer, 'the court has found you guilty of murdering Dr. So-and-so, and has sentenced you to…'

'The chief judge meant to say "to the death penalty", but he dropped from his hands the paper on which the sentence was written, wiped the cold sweat from his face, and cried out:

'No! May God punish me if I judge wrongly, but I swear he is not guilty. I cannot admit the thought that there exists a man who would dare to murder our friend the doctor! A man could not sink so low!'

'There cannot be such a man!' the other judges assented.

'No,' the crowd cried. 'Let him go!'

'The murderer was set free to go where he chose, and not one soul blamed the court for an unjust verdict. And my grandmother used to say that for such faith in humanity God forgave the sins of all the inhabitants of that town. He rejoices when people believe that man is His image and semblance, and grieves if, forgetful of human dignity, they judge worse of men than of dogs. The sentence of acquittal may bring harm to the inhabitants of the town, but on the other hand, think of the beneficial influence upon them of that faith in man – a faith which does not remain dead, you know; it raises up generous feelings in us, and always impels us to love and respect every man. Every man! And that is important.'

Mihail Karlovitch had finished. My neighbor would have urged some objection, but the head-gardener made a gesture that signified that he did not like objections; then he walked away to the carts, and, with an expression of dignity, went on looking after the packing.

The Helpmate

'I've asked you not to tidy my table,' said Nikolay Yevgrafitch. 'There's no finding anything when you've tidied up. Where's the telegram? Where have you thrown it? Be so good as to look for it. It's from Kazan, dated yesterday.'

The maid – a pale, very slim girl with an indifferent expression – found several telegrams in the basket under the table, and handed them to the doctor without a word; but all these were telegrams from patients. Then they looked in the drawing-room, and in Olga Dmitrievna's room.

It was past midnight. Nikolay Yevgrafitch knew his wife would not be home very soon, not till five o'clock at least. He did not trust her, and when she was long away he could not sleep, was worried, and at the same time he despised his wife, and her bed, and her looking-glass, and her boxes of sweets, and the hyacinths, and the lilies of the valley which were sent her every day by someone or other, and which diffused the sickly fragrance of a florist's shop all over the house. On such nights he became petty, ill-humoured, irritable, and he fancied now that it was very necessary for him to have the telegram he had received the day before from his brother, though it contained nothing but Christmas greetings.

On the table of his wife's room under the box of stationery he found a telegram, and glanced at it casually. It was addressed to his wife, care of his mother-in-law, from Monte Carlo, and signed Michel… The doctor did not understand one word of it, as it was in some foreign language, apparently English.

'Who is this Michel? Why Monte Carlo? Why directed care of her mother?'

During the seven years of his married life he had grown used to being suspicious, guessing, catching at clues, and it had several times occurred to him, that his exercise at home had qualified him to become an excellent detective. Going into his study and beginning to reflect, he recalled at once how he had been with his wife in Petersburg a year and a half ago, and had lunched with an old school-fellow, a civil engineer, and how that engineer had introduced to him and his wife a young man of two or three and twenty, called Mihail Ivanovitch, with rather a curious short surname – Riss. Two months later the doctor had seen the young man's photograph in his wife's album, with an inscription in French: 'In remembrance of the present and in hope of the future.' Later on he had met the young man himself at his mother-in-law's. And that was at the time when his wife had taken to being very often absent and coming home at four or five o'clock in the morning, and was constantly asking him to get her a passport for abroad, which he kept refusing to do; and a continual feud went on in the house which made him feel ashamed to face the servants.

Six months before, his colleagues had decided that he was going into consumption, and advised him to throw up everything and go to the Crimea. When she heard of this, Olga Dmitrievna affected to be very much alarmed; she began to be affectionate to her husband, and kept assuring him that it would be cold and dull in the Crimea, and that he had much better go to Nice, and that she would go with him, and there would nurse him, look after him, take care of him.

Now, he understood why his wife was so particularly anxious to go to Nice: her Michel lived at Monte Carlo.

He took an English dictionary, and translating the words, and guessing their meaning, by degrees he put together the following sentence: 'I drink to the health of my beloved darling, and kiss her little foot a thousand times, and am impatiently expecting her arrival.' He pictured the pitiable, ludicrous part he would play if he had agreed to go to Nice with his wife. He felt so mortified that he almost shed tears and began pacing to and fro through all the rooms of the flat in great agitation. His pride, his plebeian fastidiousness, was revolted. Clenching his fists and scowling with disgust, he wondered how he, the son of a village priest, brought up in a clerical school, a plain, straightforward man, a surgeon by profession – how could he have let himself be enslaved, have sunk into such shameful bondage to this weak, worthless, mercenary, low creature.

'Little foot'!' he muttered to himself, crumpling up the telegram; 'little foot'!'

Of the time when he fell in love and proposed to her, and the seven years that he had been living with her, all that remained in his memory was her long, fragrant hair, a mass of soft lace, and her little feet, which certainly were very small, beautiful feet; and even now it seemed as though he still had from those old embraces the feeling of lace and silk upon his hands and face – and nothing more. Nothing more – that is, not counting hysterics, shrieks, reproaches, threats, and lies – brazen, treacherous lies. He remembered how in his father's house in the village a bird would sometimes chance to fly in from the open air into the house and would struggle desperately against the window-panes and upset things; so this woman from a class utterly alien to him had flown into his life and made complete havoc of it. The best years of his life had been spent as though in hell, his hopes for happiness shattered and turned into a mockery, his health gone, his rooms as vulgar in their atmosphere as a cocotte's, and of the ten thousand he earned every year he could never save ten roubles to send his old mother in the village, and his debts were already about fifteen thousand. It seemed that if a band of brigands had been living in his rooms his life would not have been so hopelessly, so irremediably ruined as by the presence of this woman.

He began coughing and gasping for breath. He ought to have gone to bed and got warm, but he could not. He kept walking about the rooms, or sat down to the table, nervously fidgeting with a pencil and scribbling mechanically on a paper.

'Trying a pen… A little foot.'

By five o'clock he grew weaker and threw all the blame on himself. It seemed to him now that if Olga Dmitrievna had married someone else who might have had a good influence over her – who knows? – she might after all have become a good, straightforward woman. He was a poor psychologist, and knew nothing of the female heart; besides, he was churlish, uninteresting…

'I haven't long to live now,' he thought. 'I am a dead man, and ought not to stand in the way of the living. It would be strange and stupid to insist upon one's rights now. I'll have it out with her; let her go to the man she loves… I'll give her a divorce. I'll take the blame on myself.'

Olga Dmitrievna came in at last, and she walked into the study and sank into a chair just as she was in her white cloak, hat, and overboots.

'The nasty, fat boy,' she said with a sob, breathing hard. 'It's really dishonest; it's disgusting.' She stamped. 'I can't put up with it; I can't, I can't!'

'What's the matter?' asked Nikolay Yevgrafitch, going up to her.

'That student, Azarbekov, was seeing me home, and he lost my bag, and there was fifteen roubles in it. I borrowed it from mamma.'

She was crying in a most genuine way, like a little girl, and not only her handkerchief, but even her gloves, were wet with tears.

'It can't be helped!' said the doctor. 'If he's lost it, he's lost it, and it's no good worrying over it. Calm yourself; I want to talk to you.'

'I am not a millionaire to lose money like that. He says he'll pay it back, but I don't believe him; he's poor…'

Her husband begged her to calm herself and to listen to him, but she kept on talking of the student and of the fifteen roubles she had lost.

'Ach! I'll give you twenty-five roubles tomorrow if you'll only hold your tongue!' he said irritably.

'I must take off my things!' she said, crying. 'I can't talk seriously in my fur coat! How strange you are!'

He helped her off with her coat and overboots, detecting as he did so the smell of the white wine she liked to drink with oysters (in spite of her etherealness she ate and drank a great deal). She went into her room and came back soon after, having changed her things and powdered her face, though her eyes still showed traces of tears. She sat down, retreating into her light, lacy dressing-gown, and in the mass of billowy pink her husband could see nothing but her hair, which she had let down, and her little foot wearing a slipper.

'What do you want to talk about?' she asked, swinging herself in a rocking-chair.

'I happened to see this;' and he handed her the telegram.

She read it and shrugged her shoulders.

'Well?' she said, rocking herself faster. 'That's the usual New Year's greeting and nothing else. There are no secrets in it.'

'You are reckoning on my not knowing English. No, I don't know it; but I have a dictionary. That telegram is from Riss; he drinks to the health of his beloved and sends you a thousand kisses. But let us leave that,' the doctor went on hurriedly. 'I don't in the least want to reproach you or make a scene. We've had scenes and reproaches enough; it's time to make an end of them… This is what I want to say to you: you are free, and can live as you like.'

There was a silence. She began crying quietly.

'I set you free from the necessity of lying and keeping up pretences,' Nikolay Yevgrafitch continued. 'If you love that young man, love him; if you want to go abroad to him, go. You are young, healthy, and I am a wreck, and haven't long to live. In short… you understand me.'

He was agitated and could not go on. Olga Dmitrievna, crying and speaking in a voice of self-pity, acknowledged that she loved Riss, and used to drive out of town with him and see him in his rooms, and now she really did long to go abroad.

'You see, I hide nothing from you,' she added, with a sigh. 'My whole soul lies open before you. And I beg you again, be generous, get me a passport.'

'I repeat, you are free.'

She moved to another seat nearer him to look at the expression of his face. She did not believe him and wanted now to understand his secret meaning. She never did believe any one, and however generous were their intentions, she always suspected some petty or ignoble motive or selfish object in them. And when she looked searchingly into his face, it seemed to him that there was a gleam of green light in her eyes as in a cat's.

'When shall I get the passport?' she asked softly.

He suddenly had an impulse to say 'Never'; but he restrained himself and said:

'When you like.'

'I shall only go for a month.'

'You'll go to Riss for good. I'll get you a divorce, take the blame on myself, and Riss can marry you.'

'But I don't want a divorce!' Olga Dmitrievna retorted quickly, with an astonished face. 'I am not asking you for a divorce! Get me a passport, that's all.'

'But why don't you want the divorce?' asked the doctor, beginning to feel irritated. 'You are a strange woman. How strange you are! If you are fond of him in earnest and he loves you too, in your position you can do nothing better than get married. Can you really hesitate between marriage and adultery?'

'I understand you,' she said, walking away from him, and a spiteful, vindictive expression came into her face. 'I understand you perfectly. You are sick of me, and you simply want to get rid of me, to force this divorce on me. Thank you very much; I am not such a fool as you think. I won't accept the divorce and I won't leave you – I won't, I won't! To begin with, I don't want to lose my position in society,' she continued quickly, as though afraid of being prevented from speaking. 'Secondly, I am twenty-seven and Riss is only twenty-three; he'll be tired of me in a year and throw me over. And what's more, if you care to know, I'm not certain that my feeling will last long… so there! I'm not going to leave you.'

'Then I'll turn you out of the house!' shouted Nikolay Yevgrafitch, stamping. 'I shall turn you out, you vile, loathsome woman!'

'We shall see!' she said, and went out.

It was broad daylight outside, but the doctor still sat at the table moving the pencil over the paper and writing mechanically.

'My dear Sir… Little foot.'

Or he walked about and stopped in the drawing-room before a photograph taken seven years ago, soon after his marriage, and looked at it for a long time. It was a family group: his father-in-law, his mother-in-law, his wife Olga Dmitrievna when she was twenty, and himself in the rôle of a happy young husband. His father-in-law, a clean-shaven, dropsical privy councillor, crafty and avaricious; his mother-in-law, a stout lady with small predatory features like a weasel, who loved her daughter to distraction and helped her in everything; if her daughter were strangling someone, the mother would not have protested, but would only have screened her with her skirts. Olga Dmitrievna, too, had small predatory-looking features, but more expressive and bolder than her mother's; she was not a weasel, but a beast on a bigger scale! And Nikolay Yevgrafitch himself in the photograph looked such a guileless soul, such a kindly, good fellow, so open and simple-hearted; his whole face was relaxed in the naïve, good-natured smile of a divinity student, and he had had the simplicity to believe that that company of beasts of prey into which destiny had chanced to thrust him would give him romance and happiness and all he had dreamed of when as a student he used to sing the song 'Youth is wasted, life is nought, when the heart is cold and loveless.'

And once more he asked himself in perplexity how he, the son of a village priest, with his democratic bringing up – a plain, blunt, straightforward man – could have so helplessly surrendered to the power of this worthless, false, vulgar, petty creature, whose nature was so utterly alien to him.

When at eleven o'clock he put on his coat to go to the hospital the servant came into his study.

'What is it?' he asked.

'The mistress has got up and asks you for the twenty-five roubles you promised her yesterday.'

The Man in a Case

At the furthest end of the village of Mironositskoe some belated sportsmen lodged for the night in the elder Prokofy's barn. There were two of them, the veterinary surgeon Ivan Ivanovitch and the schoolmaster Burkin. Ivan Ivanovitch had a rather strange double-barrelled surname – Tchimsha-Himalaisky – which did not suit him at all, and he was called simply Ivan Ivanovitch all over the province. He lived at a stud-farm near the town, and had come out shooting now to get a breath of fresh air. Burkin, the high-school teacher, stayed every summer at Count P—'s, and had been thoroughly at home in this district for years.

They did not sleep. Ivan Ivanovitch, a tall, lean old fellow with long moustaches, was sitting outside the door, smoking a pipe in the moonlight. Burkin was lying within on the hay, and could not be seen in the darkness.

They were telling each other all sorts of stories. Among other things, they spoke of the fact that the elder's wife, Mavra, a healthy and by no means stupid woman, had never been beyond her native village, had never seen a town nor a railway in her life, and had spent the last ten years sitting behind the stove, and only at night going out into the street.

'What is there wonderful in that!' said Burkin. 'There are plenty of people in the world, solitary by temperament, who try to retreat into their shell like a hermit crab or a snail. Perhaps it is an instance of atavism, a return to the period when the ancestor of man was not yet a social animal and lived alone in his den, or perhaps it is only one of the diversities of human character – who knows? I am not a natural science man, and it is not my business to settle such questions; I only mean to say that people like Mavra are not uncommon. There is no need to look far; two months ago a man called Byelikov, a colleague of mine, the Greek master, died in our town. You have heard of him, no doubt. He was remarkable for always wearing goloshes and a warm wadded coat, and carrying an umbrella even in the very finest weather. And his umbrella was in a case, and his watch was in a case made of grey chamois leather, and when he took out his penknife to sharpen his pencil, his penknife, too, was in a little case; and his face seemed to be in a case too, because he always hid it in his turned-up collar. He wore dark spectacles and flannel vests, stuffed up his ears with cotton-wool, and when he got into a cab always told the driver to put up the hood. In short, the man displayed a constant and insurmountable impulse to wrap himself in a covering, to make himself, so to speak, a case which would isolate him and protect him from external influences. Reality irritated him, frightened him, kept him in continual agitation, and, perhaps to justify his timidity, his aversion for the actual, he always praised the past and what had never existed; and even the classical languages which he taught were in reality for him goloshes and umbrellas in which he sheltered himself from real life.

'Oh, how sonorous, how beautiful is the Greek language!' he would say, with a sugary expression; and as though to prove his words he would screw up his eyes and, raising his finger, would pronounce 'Anthropos!'

'And Byelikov tried to hide his thoughts also in a case. The only things that were clear to his mind were government circulars and newspaper articles in which something was forbidden. When some proclamation prohibited the boys from going out in the streets after nine o'clock in the evening, or some article declared carnal love unlawful, it was to his mind clear and definite; it was forbidden, and that was enough. For him there was always a doubtful element, something vague and not fully expressed, in any sanction or permission. When a dramatic club or a reading-room or a tea-shop was licensed in the town, he would shake his head and say softly:

'It is all right, of course; it is all very nice, but I hope it won't lead to anything!'

'Every sort of breach of order, deviation or departure from rule, depressed him, though one would have thought it was no business of his. If one of his colleagues was late for church or if rumours reached him of some prank of the high-school boys, or one of the mistresses was seen late in the evening in the company of an officer, he was much disturbed, and said he hoped that nothing would come of it. At the teachers' meetings he simply oppressed us with his caution, his circumspection, and his characteristic reflection on the ill-behaviour of the young people in both male and female high-schools, the uproar in the classes.

'Oh, he hoped it would not reach the ears of the authorities; oh, he hoped nothing would come of it; and he thought it would be a very good thing if Petrov were expelled from the second class and Yegorov from the fourth. And, do you know, by his sighs, his despondency, his black spectacles on his pale little face, a little face like a pole-cat's, you know, he crushed us all, and we gave way, reduced Petrov's and Yegorov's marks for conduct, kept them in, and in the end expelled them both. He had a strange habit of visiting our lodgings. He would come to a teacher's, would sit down, and remain silent, as though he were carefully inspecting something. He would sit like this in silence for an hour or two and then go away. This he called 'maintaining good relations with his colleagues'; and it was obvious that coming to see us and sitting there was tiresome to him, and that he came to see us simply because he considered it his duty as our colleague. We teachers were afraid of him. And even the headmaster was afraid of him. Would you believe it, our teachers were all intellectual, right-minded people, brought up on Turgenev and Shtchedrin, yet this little chap, who always went about with goloshes and an umbrella, had the whole high-school under his thumb for fifteen long years! High-school, indeed – he had the whole town under his thumb! Our ladies did not get up private theatricals on Saturdays for fear he should hear of it, and the clergy dared not eat meat or play cards in his presence. Under the influence of people like Byelikov we have got into the way of being afraid of everything in our town for the last ten or fifteen years. They are afraid to speak aloud, afraid to send letters, afraid to make acquaintances, afraid to read books, afraid to help the poor, to teach people to read and write…'

Ivan Ivanovitch cleared his throat, meaning to say something, but first lighted his pipe, gazed at the moon, and then said, with pauses:

'Yes, intellectual, right minded people read Shtchedrin and Turgenev, Buckle, and all the rest of them, yet they knocked under and put up with it… that's just how it is.'

'Byelikov lived in the same house as I did,' Burkin went on, 'on the same storey, his door facing mine; we often saw each other, and I knew how he lived when he was at home. And at home it was the same story: dressing-gown, nightcap, blinds, bolts, a perfect succession of prohibitions and restrictions of all sorts, and – 'Oh, I hope nothing will come of it!' Lenten fare was bad for him, yet he could not eat meat, as people might perhaps say Byelikov did not keep the fasts, and he ate freshwater fish with butter – not a Lenten dish, yet one could not say that it was meat. He did not keep a female servant for fear people might think evil of him, but had as cook an old man of sixty, called Afanasy, half-witted and given to tippling, who had once been an officer's servant and could cook after a fashion. This Afanasy was usually standing at the door with his arms folded; with a deep sigh, he would mutter always the same thing:

'There are plenty of *them* about nowadays!'

'Byelikov had a little bedroom like a box; his bed had curtains. When he went to bed he covered his head over; it was hot and stuffy; the wind battered on the closed doors; there was a droning noise in the stove and a sound of sighs from the kitchen – ominous sighs… And he felt frightened under the bed-clothes. He was afraid that something might happen, that Afanasy might murder him, that thieves might break in, and so he had troubled dreams all night, and in the morning, when we went together to the high-school, he was depressed and pale, and it was evident that the high-school full of people excited dread and aversion in his whole being, and that to walk beside me was irksome to a man of his solitary temperament.

'They make a great noise in our classes,' he used to say, as though trying to find an explanation for his depression. 'It's beyond anything.'

'And the Greek master, this man in a case – would you believe it? – almost got married.'

Ivan Ivanovitch glanced quickly into the barn, and said:

'You are joking!'

'Yes, strange as it seems, he almost got married. A new teacher of history and geography, Milhail Savvitch Kovalenko, a Little Russian, was appointed. He came, not alone, but with his sister Varinka. He was a tall, dark young man with huge hands, and one could see from his face that he had a bass voice, and, in fact, he had a voice that seemed to come out of a barrel – 'boom, boom, boom!' And she was not so young, about thirty, but she, too, was tall, well-made, with black eyebrows and red cheeks – in fact, she was a regular sugar-plum, and so sprightly, so noisy; she was always singing Little Russian songs and laughing. For the least thing she would go off into a ringing laugh – 'Ha-ha-ha!' We made our first thorough acquaintance with the Kovalenkos at the headmaster's name-day party. Among the glum and intensely bored teachers who came even to the name-day party as a duty we suddenly saw a new Aphrodite risen from the waves; she walked with her arms akimbo, laughed, sang, danced… She sang with feeling 'The Winds do Blow,' then another song, and another, and she fascinated us all – all, even Byelikov. He sat down by her and said with a honeyed smile:

'The Little Russian reminds one of the ancient Greek in its softness and agreeable resonance.'

'That flattered her, and she began telling him with feeling and earnestness that they had a farm in the Gadyatchsky district, and that her mamma lived at the farm, and that they had such pears, such melons, such *kabaks!* The Little Russians call pumpkins *kabaks* (i.e., pothouses), while their pothouses they call *shinki*, and they make a beetroot soup with tomatoes and aubergines in it, 'which was so nice – awfully nice!'

'We listened and listened, and suddenly the same idea dawned upon us all:

'It would be a good thing to make a match of it,' the headmaster's wife said to me softly.

'We all for some reason recalled the fact that our friend Byelikov was not married, and it now seemed to us strange that we had hitherto failed to observe, and had in fact completely lost sight of, a detail so important in his life. What was his attitude to woman? How had he settled this vital question for himself? This had not interested us in the least till then; perhaps we had not even admitted the idea that a man who went out in all weathers in goloshes and slept under curtains could be in love.

'He is a good deal over forty and she is thirty,' the headmaster's wife went on, developing her idea. 'I believe she would marry him.'

'All sorts of things are done in the provinces through boredom, all sorts of unnecessary and nonsensical things! And that is because what is necessary is not done at all. What need was there for instance, for us to make a match for this Byelikov, whom one could not even imagine married? The headmaster's wife, the inspector's wife, and all our high-school ladies, grew livelier and even better-looking, as though they had suddenly found a new object in life. The headmaster's wife would take a box at the theatre, and we beheld sitting in her box Varinka, with such a fan, beaming and happy, and beside her Byelikov, a little bent figure, looking as though he had been extracted from his house by pincers. I would give an evening party, and the ladies would insist on my inviting Byelikov and Varinka. In short, the machine was set in motion. It appeared that Varinka was not averse to matrimony. She had not a very cheerful life with her brother; they could do nothing but quarrel and scold one another from morning till night. Here is a scene, for instance. Kovalenko would be coming along the street, a tall, sturdy young ruffian, in an embroidered shirt, his love-locks falling on his forehead under his cap, in one hand a bundle of books, in the other a thick knotted stick, followed by his sister, also with books in her hand.

'But you haven't read it, Mihalik!' she would be arguing loudly. 'I tell you, I swear you have not read it at all!'

'And I tell you I have read it,' cries Kovalenko, thumping his stick on the pavement.

'Oh, my goodness, Mihalik! why are you so cross? We are arguing about principles.'

'I tell you that I have read it!' Kovalenko would shout, more loudly than ever.

'And at home, if there was an outsider present, there was sure to be a skirmish. Such a life must have been wearisome, and of course she must have longed for a home of her own. Besides, there was her age to be considered; there was no time left to pick and choose; it was a case of marrying anybody, even a Greek master. And, indeed, most of our young ladies don't mind whom they marry so long as they do get married. However that may be, Varinka began to show an unmistakable partiality for Byelikov.

'And Byelikov? He used to visit Kovalenko just as he did us. He would arrive, sit down, and remain silent. He would sit quiet, and Varinka would sing to him 'The Winds do Blow,' or would look pensively at him with her dark eyes, or would suddenly go off into a peal – 'Ha-ha-ha!'

'Suggestion plays a great part in love affairs, and still more in getting married. Everybody – both his colleagues and the ladies – began assuring Byelikov that he ought to get married, that there was nothing left for him in life but to get married; we all congratulated him, with solemn countenances delivered ourselves of various platitudes, such as 'Marriage is a serious step.' Besides, Varinka was good-looking and interesting; she was the daughter of a civil councillor, and had a farm; and what was more, she was the first woman who had been warm and friendly in her manner to him. His head was turned, and he decided that he really ought to get married.'

'Well, at that point you ought to have taken away his goloshes and umbrella,' said Ivan Ivanovitch.

'Only fancy! that turned out to be impossible. He put Varinka's portrait on his table, kept coming to see me and talking about Varinka, and home life, saying marriage was a serious step. He was frequently at Kovalenko's, but he did not alter his manner of life in the least; on the contrary, indeed, his determination to get married seemed to have a depressing effect on him. He grew thinner and paler, and seemed to retreat further and further into his case.

"'I like Varvara Savvishna," he used to say to me, with a faint and wry smile, "and I know that everyone ought to get married, but … you know all this has happened so suddenly… One must think a little."

"'What is there to think over?" I used to say to him. "Get married – that is all."

"'No; marriage is a serious step. One must first weigh the duties before one, the responsibilities… that nothing may go wrong afterwards. It worries me so much that I don't sleep at night. And I must confess I am afraid: her brother and she have a strange way of thinking; they look at things strangely, you know, and her disposition is very impetuous. One may get married, and then, there is no knowing, one may find oneself in an unpleasant position."

'And he did not make an offer; he kept putting it off, to the great vexation of the headmaster's wife and all our ladies; he went on weighing his future duties and responsibilities, and meanwhile he went for a walk with Varinka almost every day – possibly he thought that this was necessary in his position – and came to see me to talk about family life. And in all probability in the end he would have proposed to her, and would have made one of those unnecessary, stupid marriages such as are made by thousands among us from being bored and having nothing to do, if it had not been for a *kolossalische scandal*. I must mention that Varinka's brother, Kovalenko, detested Byelikov from the first day of their acquaintance, and could not endure him.

"'I don't understand," he used to say to us, shrugging his shoulders – "I don't understand how you can put up with that sneak, that nasty phiz. Ugh! how can you live here! The atmosphere is stifling and unclean! Do you call yourselves schoolmasters, teachers? You are paltry government clerks. You keep, not a temple of science, but a department for red tape and loyal behaviour, and it smells as sour as a police-station. No, my friends; I will stay with you for a while, and then I will go to my farm and there catch crabs and teach the Little Russians. I shall go, and you can stay here with your Judas – damn his soul!"

'Or he would laugh till he cried, first in a loud bass, then in a shrill, thin laugh, and ask me, waving his hands:

'"What does he sit here for? What does he want? He sits and stares."

'He even gave Byelikov a nickname, "The Spider". And it will readily be understood that we avoided talking to him of his sister's being about to marry "The Spider".

'And on one occasion, when the headmaster's wife hinted to him what a good thing it would be to secure his sister's future with such a reliable, universally respected man as Byelikov, he frowned and muttered:

'"It's not my business; let her marry a reptile if she likes. I don't like meddling in other people's affairs."

'Now hear what happened next. Some mischievous person drew a caricature of Byelikov walking along in his goloshes with his trousers tucked up, under his umbrella, with Varinka on his arm; below, the inscription "Anthropos in love". The expression was caught to a marvel, you know. The artist must have worked for more than one night, for the teachers of both the boys' and girls' high-schools, the teachers of the seminary, the government officials, all received a copy. Byelikov received one, too. The caricature made a very painful impression on him.

'We went out together; it was the first of May, a Sunday, and all of us, the boys and the teachers, had agreed to meet at the high-school and then to go for a walk together to a wood beyond the town. We set off, and he was green in the face and gloomier than a storm-cloud.

'What wicked, ill-natured people there are!' he said, and his lips quivered.

'I felt really sorry for him. We were walking along, and all of a sudden – would you believe it? – Kovalenko came bowling along on a bicycle, and after him, also on a bicycle, Varinka, flushed and exhausted, but good-humoured and gay.

'"We are going on ahead," she called. "What lovely weather! Awfully lovely!"

'And they both disappeared from our sight. Byelikov turned white instead of green, and seemed petrified. He stopped short and stared at me...

"'What is the meaning of it? Tell me, please!" he asked. "Can my eyes have deceived me? Is it the proper thing for high-school masters and ladies to ride bicycles?"

"'What is there improper about it?' I said. 'Let them ride and enjoy themselves.'

"'But how can that be?' he cried, amazed at my calm. "What are you saying?'

'And he was so shocked that he was unwilling to go on, and returned home.

'Next day he was continually twitching and nervously rubbing his hands, and it was evident from his face that he was unwell. And he left before his work was over, for the first time in his life. And he ate no dinner. Towards evening he wrapped himself up warmly, though it was quite warm weather, and sallied out to the Kovalenkos'. Varinka was out; he found her brother, however.

"'Pray sit down," Kovalenko said coldly, with a frown. His face looked sleepy; he had just had a nap after dinner, and was in a very bad humour.

'Byelikov sat in silence for ten minutes, and then began:

"'I have come to see you to relieve my mind. I am very, very much troubled. Some scurrilous fellow has drawn an absurd caricature of me and another person, in whom we are both deeply interested. I regard it as a duty to assure you that I have had no hand in it… I have given no sort of ground for such ridicule – on the contrary, I have always behaved in every way like a gentleman."

'Kovalenko sat sulky and silent. Byelikov waited a little, and went on slowly in a mournful voice:

"'And I have something else to say to you. I have been in the service for years, while you have only lately entered it, and I consider it my duty as an older colleague to give you a warning. You ride on a bicycle, and that pastime is utterly unsuitable for an educator of youth."

"'Why so?" asked Kovalenko in his bass.

"'Surely that needs no explanation, Mihail Savvitch – surely you can understand that? If the teacher rides a bicycle, what can you expect the pupils to do? You will have them walking on their heads next! And so long as there is no formal permission to do so, it is out of the question. I was horrified yesterday! When I saw your sister everything seemed dancing before my eyes. A lady or a young girl on a bicycle – it's awful!"

"'What is it you want exactly?"

"'All I want is to warn you, Mihail Savvitch. You are a young man, you have a future before you, you must be very, very careful in your behaviour, and you are so careless – oh, so careless! You go about in an embroidered shirt, are constantly seen in the street carrying books, and now the bicycle, too. The headmaster will learn that you and your sister ride the bicycle, and then it will reach the higher authorities… Will that be a good thing?"

"'It's no business of anybody else if my sister and I do bicycle!" said Kovalenko, and he turned crimson. "And damnation take any one who meddles in my private affairs!"

'Byelikov turned pale and got up.

"'If you speak to me in that tone I cannot continue," he said. "And I beg you never to express yourself like that about our superiors in my presence; you ought to be respectful to the authorities."

"'Why, have I said any harm of the authorities?" asked Kovalenko, looking at him wrathfully. "Please leave me alone. I am an honest man, and do not care to talk to a gentleman like you. I don't like sneaks!"

'Byelikov flew into a nervous flutter, and began hurriedly putting on his coat, with an expression of horror on his face. It was the first time in his life he had been spoken to so rudely.

"'You can say what you please," he said, as he went out from the entry to the landing on the staircase. "I ought only to warn you: possibly someone may have overheard us, and that our conversation may not be misunderstood and harm come of it, I shall be compelled to inform our headmaster of our conversation… in its main features. I am bound to do so."

"'Inform him? You can go and make your report!"

'Kovalenko seized him from behind by the collar and gave him a push, and Byelikov rolled downstairs, thudding with his galoshes. The staircase was high and steep, but he rolled to the bottom unhurt, got up, and touched his nose to see whether his spectacles were all right. But just as he was falling down the stairs Varinka came in, and with her two ladies; they stood below staring, and to Byelikov this was more terrible than anything. I believe he would rather have broken his neck or both legs than have been an object of ridicule. "Why, now the whole town would hear of it; it would come to the headmaster's ears, would reach the higher authorities – oh, it might lead to something! There would be another caricature, and it would all end in his being asked to resign his post…

'When he got up, Varinka recognized him, and, looking at his ridiculous face, his crumpled overcoat, and his goloshes, not understanding what had happened and supposing that he had slipped down by accident, could not restrain herself, and laughed loud enough to be heard by all the flats:

'"Ha-ha-ha!"

'And this pealing, ringing "Ha-ha-ha!" was the last straw that put an end to everything: to the proposed match and to Byelikov's earthly existence. He did not hear what Varinka said to him; he saw nothing. On reaching home, the first thing he did was to remove her portrait from the table; then he went to bed, and he never got up again.

'Three days later Afanasy came to me and asked whether we should not send for the doctor, as there was something wrong with his master. I went in to Byelikov. He lay silent behind the curtain, covered with a quilt; if one asked him a question, he said "Yes" or "No" and not another sound. He lay there while Afanasy, gloomy and scowling, hovered about him, sighing heavily, and smelling like a pothouse.

'A month later Byelikov died. We all went to his funeral – that is, both the high-schools and the seminary. Now when he was lying in his coffin his expression was mild, agreeable, even cheerful, as though he were glad that he had at last been put into a case which he would never leave again. Yes, he had attained his ideal! And, as though in his honour, it was dull, rainy weather on the day of his funeral, and we all wore goloshes and took our umbrellas. Varinka, too, was at the funeral, and when the coffin was lowered into the grave she burst into tears. I have noticed that Little Russian women are always laughing or crying – no intermediate mood.

'One must confess that to bury people like Byelikov is a great pleasure. As we were returning from the cemetery we wore discreet

Lenten faces; no one wanted to display this feeling of pleasure – a feeling like that we had experienced long, long ago as children when our elders had gone out and we ran about the garden for an hour or two, enjoying complete freedom. Ah, freedom, freedom! The merest hint, the faintest hope of its possibility gives wings to the soul, does it not?

'We returned from the cemetery in a good humour. But not more than a week had passed before life went on as in the past, as gloomy, oppressive, and senseless – a life not forbidden by government prohibition, but not fully permitted, either: it was no better. And, indeed, though we had buried Byelikov, how many such men in cases were left, how many more of them there will be!'

'That's just how it is,' said Ivan Ivanovitch and he lighted his pipe.

'How many more of them there will be!' repeated Burkin.

The schoolmaster came out of the barn. He was a short, stout man, completely bald, with a black beard down to his waist. The two dogs came out with him.

'What a moon!' he said, looking upwards.

It was midnight. On the right could be seen the whole village, a long street stretching far away for four miles. All was buried in deep silent slumber; not a movement, not a sound; one could hardly believe that nature could be so still. When on a moonlight night you see a broad village street, with its cottages, haystacks, and slumbering willows, a feeling of calm comes over the soul; in this peace, wrapped away from care, toil, and sorrow in the darkness of night, it is mild, melancholy, beautiful, and it seems as though the stars look down upon it kindly and with tenderness, and as though there were no evil on earth and all were well. On the left the open country began from the end of the village; it could be seen stretching far away to the horizon, and there was no movement, no sound in that whole expanse bathed in moonlight.

'Yes, that is just how it is,' repeated Ivan Ivanovitch; 'and isn't our living in town, airless and crowded, our writing useless papers, our playing *vint* – isn't that all a sort of case for us? And our spending our whole lives among trivial, fussy men and silly, idle women, our talking and our listening to all sorts of nonsense – isn't that a case for us, too? If you like, I will tell you a very edifying story.'

'No; it's time we were asleep,' said Burkin. 'Tell it tomorrow.'

They went into the barn and lay down on the hay. And they were both covered up and beginning to doze when they suddenly heard light footsteps – patter, patter… Someone was walking not far from the barn, walking a little and stopping, and a minute later, patter, patter again… The dogs began growling.

'That's Mavra,' said Burkin.

The footsteps died away.

'You see and hear that they lie,' said Ivan Ivanovitch, turning over on the other side, 'and they call you a fool for putting up with their lying. You endure insult and humiliation, and dare not openly say that you are on the side of the honest and the free, and you lie and smile yourself; and all that for the sake of a crust of bread, for the sake of a warm corner, for the sake of a wretched little worthless rank in the service. No, one can't go on living like this.'

'Well, you are off on another tack now, Ivan Ivanovitch,' said the schoolmaster. 'Let us go to sleep!'

And ten minutes later Burkin was asleep. But Ivan Ivanovitch kept sighing and turning over from side to side; then he got up, went outside again, and, sitting in the doorway, lighted his pipe.

Gooseberries

The whole sky had been overcast with rain-clouds from early morning; it was a still day, not hot, but heavy, as it is in grey dull weather when the clouds have been hanging over the country for a long while, when one expects rain and it does not come. Ivan Ivanovitch, the veterinary surgeon, and Burkin, the high-school teacher, were already tired from walking, and the fields seemed to them endless. Far ahead of them they could just see the windmills of the village of Mironositskoe; on the right stretched a row of hillocks which disappeared in the distance behind the village, and they both knew that this was the bank of the river, that there were meadows, green willows, homesteads there, and that if one stood on one of the hillocks one could see from it the same vast plain, telegraph-wires, and a train which in the distance looked like a crawling caterpillar, and that in clear weather one could even see the town. Now, in still weather, when all nature seemed mild and dreamy, Ivan Ivanovitch and Burkin were filled with love of that countryside, and both thought how great, how beautiful a land it was.

'Last time we were in Prokofy's barn,' said Burkin, 'you were about to tell me a story.'

'Yes; I meant to tell you about my brother.'

Ivan Ivanovitch heaved a deep sigh and lighted a pipe to begin to tell his story, but just at that moment the rain began. And five minutes later heavy rain came down, covering the sky, and it was hard to tell when it would be over. Ivan Ivanovitch and Burkin stopped in hesitation; the dogs, already drenched, stood with their tails between their legs gazing at them feelingly.

'We must take shelter somewhere,' said Burkin. 'Let us go to Alehin's; it's close by.'

'Come along.'

They turned aside and walked through mown fields, sometimes going straight forward, sometimes turning to the right, till they came out on the road. Soon they saw poplars, a garden, then the red roofs of barns; there was a gleam of the river, and the view opened on to a broad expanse of water with a windmill and a white bath-house: this was Sofino, where Alehin lived.

The watermill was at work, drowning the sound of the rain; the dam was shaking. Here wet horses with drooping heads were standing near their carts, and men were walking about covered with sacks. It was damp, muddy, and desolate; the water looked cold and malignant. Ivan Ivanovitch and Burkin were already conscious of a feeling of wetness, messiness, and discomfort all over; their feet were heavy with mud, and when, crossing the dam, they went up to the barns, they were silent, as though they were angry with one another.

In one of the barns there was the sound of a winnowing machine, the door was open, and clouds of dust were coming from it. In the doorway was standing Alehin himself, a man of forty, tall and stout, with long hair, more like a professor or an artist than a landowner. He had on a white shirt that badly needed washing, a rope for a belt, drawers instead of trousers, and his boots, too, were plastered up with mud and straw. His eyes and nose were black with dust. He recognized Ivan Ivanovitch and Burkin, and was apparently much delighted to see them.

'Go into the house, gentlemen,' he said, smiling; 'I'll come directly, this minute.'

It was a big two-storeyed house. Alehin lived in the lower storey, with arched ceilings and little windows, where the bailiffs had once lived; here everything was plain, and there was a smell of rye bread, cheap vodka, and harness. He went upstairs into the best rooms only on rare occasions, when visitors came. Ivan Ivanovitch and Burkin were met in the house by a maid-servant, a young woman so beautiful that they both stood still and looked at one another.

'You can't imagine how delighted I am to see you, my friends,' said Alehin, going into the hall with them. 'It is a surprise! Pelagea,' he said, addressing the girl, 'give our visitors something to change into. And, by the way, I will change too. Only I must first go and wash, for I almost think I have not washed since spring. Wouldn't you like to come into the bath-house? and meanwhile they will get things ready here.'

Beautiful Pelagea, looking so refined and soft, brought them towels and soap, and Alehin went to the bath-house with his guests.

'It's a long time since I had a wash,' he said, undressing. 'I have got a nice bath-house, as you see – my father built it – but I somehow never have time to wash.'

He sat down on the steps and soaped his long hair and his neck, and the water round him turned brown.

'Yes, I must say,' said Ivan Ivanovitch meaningly, looking at his head.

'It's a long time since I washed…' said Alehin with embarrassment, giving himself a second soaping, and the water near him turned dark blue, like ink.

Ivan Ivanovitch went outside, plunged into the water with a loud splash, and swam in the rain, flinging his arms out wide. He stirred the water into waves which set the white lilies bobbing up and down; he swam to the very middle of the millpond and dived, and came up a minute later in another place, and swam on, and kept on diving, trying to touch the bottom.

'Oh, my goodness!' he repeated continually, enjoying himself thoroughly. 'Oh, my goodness!' He swam to the mill, talked to the peasants there, then returned and lay on his back in the middle of the pond, turning his face to the rain. Burkin and Alehin were dressed and ready to go, but he still went on swimming and diving. 'Oh, my goodness!…' he said. 'Oh, Lord, have mercy on me!…'

'That's enough!' Burkin shouted to him.

They went back to the house. And only when the lamp was lighted in the big drawing-room upstairs, and Burkin and Ivan Ivanovitch, attired in silk dressing-gowns and warm slippers, were sitting in arm-chairs; and Alehin, washed and combed, in a new coat, was walking about the drawing-room, evidently enjoying the feeling of warmth, cleanliness, dry clothes, and light shoes; and when lovely Pelagea, stepping noiselessly on the carpet and smiling softly, handed tea and jam on a tray – only then Ivan Ivanovitch began on his story, and it seemed as though not only Burkin and Alehin were listening, but also the ladies, young and old, and the officers who looked down upon them sternly and calmly from their gold frames.

'There are two of us brothers,' he began – 'I, Ivan Ivanovitch, and my brother, Nikolay Ivanovitch, two years younger. I went in for a learned profession and became a veterinary surgeon, while Nikolay sat in a government office from the time he was nineteen. Our father, Tchimsha-Himalaisky, was a kantonist, but he rose to be an officer and left us a little estate and the rank of nobility. After his death the little estate went in debts and legal expenses; but, anyway, we had spent our childhood running wild in the country. Like peasant children, we passed our days and nights in the fields and the woods, looked after horses, stripped the bark off the trees, fished, and so on… And, you know, whoever has once in his life caught perch or has seen the migrating of the thrushes in autumn, watched how they float in flocks over the village on bright, cool days, he will never be a real townsman, and will have a yearning for freedom to the day of his death. My brother was miserable in the government office. Years passed by, and he went on sitting in the same place, went on writing the same papers and thinking of one and the same thing – how to get into the country. And this yearning by degrees passed into a definite desire, into a dream of buying himself a little farm somewhere on the banks of a river or a lake.

'He was a gentle, good-natured fellow, and I was fond of him, but I never sympathized with this desire to shut himself up for the rest of his life in a little farm of his own. It's the correct thing to say that a man needs no more than six feet of earth. But six feet is what a corpse needs, not a man. And they say, too, now, that if our intellectual classes are attracted to the land and yearn for a farm, it's a good thing. But these farms are just the same as six feet of earth. To retreat from town, from the struggle, from the bustle of life, to retreat and bury oneself in one's farm – it's not life, it's egoism, laziness, it's monasticism of a sort, but monasticism without good works. A man does not need six feet of earth or a farm, but the whole globe, all nature, where he can have room to display all the qualities and peculiarities of his free spirit.

'My brother Nikolay, sitting in his government office, dreamed of how he would eat his own cabbages, which would fill the whole yard with such a savoury smell, take his meals on the green grass, sleep in the sun, sit for whole hours on the seat by the gate gazing at the fields and the forest. Gardening books and the agricultural hints in calendars were his delight, his favourite spiritual sustenance; he enjoyed reading newspapers, too, but the only things he read in them were the advertisements of so many acres of arable land and a grass meadow with farm-houses and buildings, a river, a garden, a mill and millponds, for sale. And his imagination pictured the garden-paths, flowers and fruit, starling cotes, the carp in the pond, and all that sort of thing, you know. These imaginary pictures were of different kinds according to the advertisements which he came across, but for some reason in every one of them he had always to have gooseberries. He could not imagine a homestead, he could not picture an idyllic nook, without gooseberries.

'"Country life has its conveniences," he would sometimes say. "You sit on the verandah and you drink tea, while your ducks swim on the pond, there is a delicious smell everywhere, and... and the gooseberries are growing."

'He used to draw a map of his property, and in every map there were the same things – (a) house for the family, (b) servants' quarters, (c) kitchen-garden, (d) gooseberry-bushes. He lived parsimoniously, was frugal in food and drink, his clothes were beyond description; he looked like a beggar, but kept on saving and putting money in the bank. He grew fearfully avaricious. I did not like to look at him, and

I used to give him something and send him presents for Christmas and Easter, but he used to save that too. Once a man is absorbed by an idea there is no doing anything with him.

'Years passed: he was transferred to another province. He was over forty, and he was still reading the advertisements in the papers and saving up. Then I heard he was married. Still with the same object of buying a farm and having gooseberries, he married an elderly and ugly widow without a trace of feeling for her, simply because she had filthy lucre. He went on living frugally after marrying her, and kept her short of food, while he put her money in the bank in his name.

'Her first husband had been a postmaster, and with him she was accustomed to pies and home-made wines, while with her second husband she did not get enough black bread; she began to pine away with this sort of life, and three years later she gave up her soul to God. And I need hardly say that my brother never for one moment imagined that he was responsible for her death. Money, like vodka, makes a man queer. In our town there was a merchant who, before he died, ordered a plateful of honey and ate up all his money and lottery tickets with the honey, so that no one might get the benefit of it. While I was inspecting cattle at a railway-station, a cattle-dealer fell under an engine and had his leg cut off. We carried him into the waiting-room, the blood was flowing – it was a horrible thing – and he kept asking them to look for his leg and was very much worried about it; there were twenty roubles in the boot on the leg that had been cut off, and he was afraid they would be lost.'

'That's a story from a different opera,' said Burkin.

'After his wife's death,' Ivan Ivanovitch went on, after thinking for half a minute, 'my brother began looking out for an estate for himself. Of course, you may look about for five years and yet end by making a mistake, and buying something quite different from what you have dreamed of. My brother Nikolay bought through an agent a mortgaged estate of three hundred and thirty acres, with a house for the family, with servants' quarters, with a park, but with no orchard, no gooseberry-bushes, and no duck-pond; there was a river, but the water in it was the colour of coffee, because on one side of the estate there was a brickyard and on the other a factory for burning bones. But Nikolay

Ivanovitch did not grieve much; he ordered twenty gooseberry-bushes, planted them, and began living as a country gentleman.

'Last year I went to pay him a visit. I thought I would go and see what it was like. In his letters my brother called his estate 'Tchumbaroklov Waste, alias Himalaiskoe.' I reached 'alias Himalaiskoe' in the afternoon. It was hot. Everywhere there were ditches, fences, hedges, fir-trees planted in rows, and there was no knowing how to get to the yard, where to put one's horse. I went up to the house, and was met by a fat red dog that looked like a pig. It wanted to bark, but it was too lazy. The cook, a fat, barefooted woman, came out of the kitchen, and she, too, looked like a pig, and said that her master was resting after dinner. I went in to see my brother. He was sitting up in bed with a quilt over his legs; he had grown older, fatter, wrinkled; his cheeks, his nose, and his mouth all stuck out – he looked as though he might begin grunting into the quilt at any moment.

'We embraced each other, and shed tears of joy and of sadness at the thought that we had once been young and now were both grey-headed and near the grave. He dressed, and led me out to show me the estate.

'"Well, how are you getting on here?" I asked.

'"Oh, all right, thank God; I am getting on very well."

'He was no more a poor timid clerk, but a real landowner, a gentleman. He was already accustomed to it, had grown used to it, and liked it. He ate a great deal, went to the bath-house, was growing stout, was already at law with the village commune and both factories, and was very much offended when the peasants did not call him 'Your Honour.' And he concerned himself with the salvation of his soul in a substantial, gentlemanly manner, and performed deeds of charity, not simply, but with an air of consequence. And what deeds of charity! He treated the peasants for every sort of disease with soda and castor oil, and on his name-day had a thanksgiving service in the middle of the village, and then treated the peasants to a gallon of vodka – he thought that was the thing to do. Oh, those horrible gallons of vodka! One day the fat landowner hauls the peasants up before the district captain for trespass, and next day, in honour of a holiday, treats them to a gallon of vodka, and they drink and shout 'Hurrah!' and when they are drunk bow down to his feet. A change of life for the better, and being well-fed and idle develop in a Russian the most insolent self-conceit. Nikolay Ivanovitch, who at one time in the government office was afraid to have any views of his own, now could say nothing that was not gospel truth, and uttered such truths in the tone of a prime minister. 'Education is essential, but for the peasants it is premature.' 'Corporal punishment is harmful as a rule, but in some cases it is necessary and there is nothing to take its place.'

"'I know the peasants and understand how to treat them," he would say. "The peasants like me. I need only to hold up my little finger and the peasants will do anything I like."

'And all this, observe, was uttered with a wise, benevolent smile. He repeated twenty times over "We noblemen," "I as a noble"; obviously he did not remember that our grandfather was a peasant, and our father a soldier. Even our surname Tchimsha-Himalaisky, in reality so incongruous, seemed to him now melodious, distinguished, and very agreeable.

'But the point just now is not he, but myself. I want to tell you about the change that took place in me during the brief hours I spent at his country place. In the evening, when we were drinking tea, the cook put on the table a plateful of gooseberries. They were not bought, but his own gooseberries, gathered for the first time since the bushes were planted. Nikolay Ivanovitch laughed and looked for a minute in silence at the gooseberries, with tears in his eyes; he could not speak for excitement. Then he put one gooseberry in his mouth, looked at me with the triumph of a child who has at last received his favourite toy, and said:

'How delicious!'

'And he ate them greedily, continually repeating, 'Ah, how delicious! Do taste them!'

'They were sour and unripe, but, as Pushkin says:

"'Dearer to us the falsehood that exalts
Than hosts of baser truths."

'I saw a happy man whose cherished dream was so obviously fulfilled, who had attained his object in life, who had gained what he wanted, who was satisfied with his fate and himself. There is always, for some reason, an element of sadness mingled with my thoughts of human happiness, and, on this occasion, at the sight of a happy man I was overcome by an oppressive feeling that was close upon despair. It was particularly oppressive at night. A bed was made up for me in the room next to my brother's bedroom, and I could hear that he was awake, and that he kept getting up and going to the plate of goose-berries and taking one. I reflected how many satisfied, happy people there really are! 'What a suffocating force it is! You look at life: the insolence and idleness of the strong, the ignorance and brutishness of the weak, incredible poverty all about us, overcrowding, degeneration, drunkenness, hypocrisy, lying… Yet all is calm and stillness in the houses and in the streets; of the fifty thousand living in a town, there is not one who would cry out, who would give vent to his indignation aloud. We see the people going to market for provisions, eating by day, sleeping by night, talking their silly nonsense, getting married, growing old, serenely escorting their dead to the cemetery; but we do not see and we do not hear those who suffer, and what is terrible in life goes on somewhere behind the scenes… Everything is quiet and peaceful, and nothing protests but mute statistics: so many people gone out of their minds, so many gallons of vodka drunk, so many children dead from malnutrition… And this order of things is evidently necessary; evidently the happy man only feels at ease because the unhappy bear their burdens in silence, and without that silence happiness would be impossible. It's a case of general hypnotism. There ought to be behind the door of every happy, contented man someone standing with a hammer continually reminding him with a tap that there are unhappy people; that however happy he may be, life will show him her laws sooner or later, trouble will come for him – disease, poverty, losses, and no one will see or hear, just as now he neither sees nor hears others. But there is no man with a hammer; the happy man lives at his ease, and trivial daily cares faintly agitate him like the wind in the aspen-tree – and all goes well.

'That night I realized that I, too, was happy and contented,' Ivan Ivanovitch went on, getting up. 'I, too, at dinner and at the hunt liked to lay down the law on life and religion, and the way to manage the peasantry. I, too, used to say that science was light, that culture was essential, but for the simple people reading and writing was enough for the time. Freedom is a blessing, I used to say; we can no more do without it than without air, but we must wait a little. Yes, I used to talk like that, and now I ask, "For what reason are we to wait?"' asked Ivan Ivanovitch, looking angrily at Burkin. 'Why wait, I ask you? What grounds have we for waiting? I shall be told, it can't be done all at once; every idea takes shape in life gradually, in its due time. But who is it says that? Where is the proof that it's right? You will fall back upon the natural order of things, the uniformity of phenomena; but is there order and uniformity in the fact that I, a living, thinking man, stand over a chasm and wait for it to close of itself, or to fill up with mud at the very time when perhaps I might leap over it or build a bridge across it? And again, wait for the sake of what? Wait till there's no strength to live? And meanwhile one must live, and one wants to live!

'I went away from my brother's early in the morning, and ever since then it has been unbearable for me to be in town. I am oppressed by its peace and quiet; I am afraid to look at the windows, for there is no spectacle more painful to me now than the sight of a happy family sitting round the table drinking tea. I am old and am not fit for the struggle; I am not even capable of hatred; I can only grieve inwardly, feel irritated and vexed; but at night my head is hot from the rush of ideas, and I cannot sleep… Ah, if I were young!'

Ivan Ivanovitch walked backwards and forwards in excitement, and repeated: 'If I were young!'

He suddenly went up to Alehin and began pressing first one of his hands and then the other.

'Pavel Konstantinovitch,' he said in an imploring voice, 'don't be calm and contented, don't let yourself be put to sleep! While you are young, strong, confident, be not weary in well-doing! There is no happiness, and there ought not to be; but if there is a meaning and an object in life, that meaning and object is not our happiness, but something greater and more rational. Do good!'

And all this Ivan Ivanovitch said with a pitiful, imploring smile, as though he were asking him a personal favour.

Then all three sat in arm-chairs at different ends of the drawing-room and were silent. Ivan Ivanovitch's story had not satisfied either Burkin or Alehin. When the generals and ladies gazed down from their gilt frames, looking in the dusk as though they were alive, it was dreary to listen to the story of the poor clerk who ate gooseberries. They felt inclined, for some reason, to talk about elegant people, about women. And their sitting in the drawing-room where everything – the chandeliers in their covers, the arm-chairs, and the carpet under their feet – reminded them that those very people who were now looking down from their frames had once moved about, sat, drunk tea in this room, and the fact that lovely Pelagea was moving noiselessly about was better than any story.

Alehin was fearfully sleepy; he had got up early, before three o'clock in the morning, to look after his work, and now his eyes were closing; but he was afraid his visitors might tell some interesting story after he had gone, and he lingered on. He did not go into the question whether what Ivan Ivanovitch had just said was right and true. His visitors did not talk of groats, nor of hay, nor of tar, but of something that had no direct bearing on his life, and he was glad and wanted them to go on.

'It's bed-time, though,' said Burkin, getting up. 'Allow me to wish you good-night.'

Alehin said goodnight and went downstairs to his own domain, while the visitors remained upstairs. They were both taken for the night to a big room where there stood two old wooden beds decorated with carvings, and in the corner was an ivory crucifix. The big cool beds, which had been made by the lovely Pelagea, smelt agreeably of clean linen.

Ivan Ivanovitch undressed in silence and got into bed.

'Lord forgive us sinners!' he said, and put his head under the quilt.

His pipe lying on the table smelt strongly of stale tobacco, and Burkin could not sleep for a long while, and kept wondering where the oppressive smell came from.

The rain was pattering on the window-panes all night.

About Love

At lunch next day there were very nice pies, crayfish, and mutton cutlets; and while we were eating, Nikanor, the cook, came up to ask what the visitors would like for dinner. He was a man of medium height, with a puffy face and little eyes; he was close-shaven, and it looked as though his moustaches had not been shaved, but had been pulled out by the roots. Alehin told us that the beautiful Pelagea was in love with this cook. As he drank and was of a violent character, she did not want to marry him, but was willing to live with him without. He was very devout, and his religious convictions would not allow him to 'live in sin'; he insisted on her marrying him, and would consent to nothing else, and when he was drunk he used to abuse her and even beat her. Whenever he got drunk she used to hide upstairs and sob, and on such occasions Alehin and the servants stayed in the house to be ready to defend her in case of necessity.

We began talking about love.

'How love is born,' said Alehin, 'why Pelagea does not love somebody more like herself in her spiritual and external qualities, and why she fell in love with Nikanor, that ugly snout – we all call him 'The Snout' – how far questions of personal happiness are of consequence in love – all that is known; one can take what view one likes of it. So far only one incontestable truth has been uttered about love: 'This is a great mystery.' Everything else that has been written or said about love is not a conclusion, but only a statement of questions which have remained unanswered. The explanation which would seem to fit one case does not apply in a dozen others, and the very best thing, to my mind, would be to explain every case individually without attempting to generalize. We ought, as the doctors say, to individualize each case.'

'Perfectly true,' Burkin assented.

'We Russians of the educated class have a partiality for these questions that remain unanswered. Love is usually poeticized, decorated with roses, nightingales; we Russians decorate our loves with these momentous questions, and select the most uninteresting of them, too. In Moscow, when I was a student, I had a friend who shared my life, a charming lady, and every time I took her in my arms she was thinking what I would allow her a month for housekeeping and what was the price of beef a pound. In the same way, when we are in love we are never tired of asking ourselves questions: whether it is honourable or dishonourable, sensible or stupid, what this love is leading up to, and so on. Whether it is a good thing or not I don't know, but that it is in the way, unsatisfactory, and irritating, I do know.'

It looked as though he wanted to tell some story. People who lead a solitary existence always have something in their hearts which they are eager to talk about. In town bachelors visit the baths and the restaurants on purpose to talk, and sometimes tell the most interesting things to bath attendants and waiters; in the country, as a rule, they unbosom themselves to their guests. Now from the window we could see a grey sky, trees drenched in the rain; in such weather we could go nowhere, and there was nothing for us to do but to tell stories and to listen.

'I have lived at Sofino and been farming for a long time,' Alehin began, 'ever since I left the University. I am an idle gentleman by education, a studious person by disposition; but there was a big debt owing on the estate when I came here, and as my father was in debt partly because he had spent so much on my education, I resolved not to go away, but to work till I paid off the debt. I made up my mind to this and set to work, not, I must confess, without some repugnance. The land here does not yield much, and if one is not to farm at a loss one must employ serf labour or hired labourers, which is almost the same thing, or put it on a peasant footing – that is, work the fields oneself and with one's family. There is no middle path. But in those days I did not go into such subtleties. I did not leave a clod of earth unturned; I gathered together all the peasants, men and women, from the neighbouring villages; the work went on at a tremendous pace. I myself ploughed and sowed and reaped, and was bored doing it, and frowned with disgust, like a village cat driven by hunger to eat cucumbers in the kitchen-garden. My body ached, and I slept as I walked. At first it seemed to me that I could easily reconcile this life of toil with my cultured habits; to do so, I thought, all that is necessary is to maintain a certain external order in life. I established myself upstairs here in the best rooms, and ordered them to bring me there coffee and liquor after lunch and dinner, and when I went to bed I read every night the *Yyesnik Evropi*. But one day our priest, Father Ivan, came and drank up all my liquor at one sitting; and the *Yyesnik Evropi* went to the priest's daughters; as in the summer, especially at the haymaking, I did not succeed in getting to my bed at all, and slept in the sledge in the barn, or somewhere in the forester's lodge, what chance was there of reading? Little by little I moved downstairs, began dining in the servants' kitchen, and of my former luxury nothing is left but the servants who were in my father's service, and whom it would be painful to turn away.

'In the first years I was elected here an honourary justice of the peace. I used to have to go to the town and take part in the sessions of the congress and of the circuit court, and this was a pleasant change for me. When you live here for two or three months without a break, especially in the winter, you begin at last to pine for a black coat. And in the circuit court there were frock-coats, and uniforms, and dress-coats, too, all lawyers, men who have received a general education; I had someone to talk to. After sleeping in the sledge and dining in the kitchen, to sit in an arm-chair in clean linen, in thin boots, with a chain on one's waistcoat, is such luxury!

'I received a warm welcome in the town. I made friends eagerly. And of all my acquaintanceships the most intimate and, to tell the truth, the most agreeable to me was my acquaintance with Luganovitch, the vice-president of the circuit court. You both know him: a most charming personality. It all happened just after a celebrated case of incendiarism; the preliminary investigation lasted two days; we were exhausted. Luganovitch looked at me and said:

"'Look here, come round to dinner with me."

'This was unexpected, as I knew Luganovitch very little, only officially, and I had never been to his house. I only just went to my hotel room to change and went off to dinner. And here it was my lot to meet Anna Alexyevna, Luganovitch's wife. At that time she was still very young, not more than twenty-two, and her first baby had been born just six months before. It is all a thing of the past; and now I should find it difficult to define what there was so exceptional in her, what it was in her attracted me so much; at the time, at dinner, it was all perfectly clear to me. I saw a lovely young, good, intelligent, fascinating woman, such as I had never met before; and I felt her at once some one close and already familiar, as though that face, those cordial, intelligent eyes, I had seen somewhere in my childhood, in the album which lay on my mother's chest of drawers.

'Four Jews were charged with being incendiaries, were regarded as a gang of robbers, and, to my mind, quite groundlessly. At dinner I was very much excited, I was uncomfortable, and I don't know what I said, but Anna Alexyevna kept shaking her head and saying to her husband:

"'Dmitry, how is this?"

'Luganovitch is a good-natured man, one of those simple-hearted people who firmly maintain the opinion that once a man is charged before a court he is guilty, and to express doubt of the correctness of a sentence cannot be done except in legal form on paper, and not at dinner and in private conversation.

"'You and I did not set fire to the place," he said softly, "and you see we are not condemned, and not in prison."

'And both husband and wife tried to make me eat and drink as much as possible. From some trifling details, from the way they made the coffee together, for instance, and from the way they understood each other at half a word, I could gather that they lived in harmony and comfort, and that they were glad of a visitor. After dinner they played a duet on the piano; then it got dark, and I went home. That was at the beginning of spring.

'After that I spent the whole summer at Sofino without a break, and I had no time to think of the town, either, but the memory of the graceful fair-haired woman remained in my mind all those days; I did not think of her, but it was as though her light shadow were lying on my heart.

'In the late autumn there was a theatrical performance for some charitable object in the town. I went into the governor's box (I was invited to go there in the interval); I looked, and there was Anna Alexyevna sitting beside the governor's wife; and again the same irresistible, thrilling impression of beauty and sweet, caressing eyes, and again the same feeling of nearness. We sat side by side, then went to the foyer.

'"You've grown thinner," she said; "have you been ill?"

'"Yes, I've had rheumatism in my shoulder, and in rainy weather I can't sleep."

'"You look dispirited. In the spring, when you came to dinner, you were younger, more confident. You were full of eagerness, and talked a great deal then; you were very interesting, and I really must confess I was a little carried away by you. For some reason you often came back to my memory during the summer, and when I was getting ready for the theatre today I thought I should see you."

'And she laughed.

'"But you look dispirited today," she repeated; "it makes you seem older."

'The next day I lunched at the Luganovitchs'. After lunch they drove out to their summer villa, in order to make arrangements there for the winter, and I went with them. I returned with them to the town, and at midnight drank tea with them in quiet domestic surroundings, while the fire glowed, and the young mother kept going to see if her baby girl was asleep. And after that, every time I went to town I never failed to visit the Luganovitchs. They grew used to me, and I grew used to them. As a rule I went in unannounced, as though I were one of the family.

'"Who is there?" I would hear from a faraway room, in the drawling voice that seemed to me so lovely.

'"It is Pavel Konstantinovitch," answered the maid or the nurse.

'Anna Alexyevna would come out to me with an anxious face, and would ask every time:

'"Why is it so long since you have been? Has anything happened?"

'Her eyes, the elegant refined hand she gave me, her indoor dress, the way she did her hair, her voice, her step, always produced the same impression on me of something new and extraordinary in my life, and very important. We talked together for hours, were silent, thinking each our own thoughts, or she played for hours to me on the piano. If there were no one at home I stayed and waited, talked to the nurse, played with the child, or lay on the sofa in the study and read; and when Anna Alexyevna came back I met her in the hall, took all her parcels from her, and for some reason I carried those parcels every time with as much love, with as much solemnity, as a boy.

'There is a proverb that if a peasant woman has no troubles she will buy a pig. The Luganovitchs had no troubles, so they made friends with me. If I did not come to the town I must be ill or something must have happened to me, and both of them were extremely anxious. They were worried that I, an educated man with a knowledge of languages, should, instead of devoting myself to science or literary work, live in the country, rush round like a squirrel in a rage, work hard with never a penny to show for it. They fancied that I was unhappy, and that I only talked, laughed, and ate to conceal my sufferings, and even at cheerful moments when I felt happy I was aware of their searching eyes fixed upon me. They were particularly touching when I really was depressed, when I was being worried by some creditor or had not money enough to pay interest on the proper day. The two of them, husband and wife, would whisper together at the window; then he would come to me and say with a grave face:

'"If you really are in need of money at the moment, Pavel

Konstantinovitch, my wife and I beg you not to hesitate to borrow from us."

'And he would blush to his ears with emotion. And it would happen that, after whispering in the same way at the window, he would come up to me, with red ears, and say:

'"My wife and I earnestly beg you to accept this present."

'And he would give me studs, a cigar-case, or a lamp, and I would send them game, butter, and flowers from the country. They both, by the way, had considerable means of their own. In early days I often borrowed money, and was not very particular about it – borrowed wherever I could – but nothing in the world would have induced me to borrow from the Luganovitchs. But why talk of it?

'I was unhappy. At home, in the fields, in the barn, I thought of her; I tried to understand the mystery of a beautiful, intelligent young woman's marrying someone so uninteresting, almost an old man (her husband was over forty), and having children by him; to understand the mystery of this uninteresting, good, simple-hearted man, who argued with such wearisome good sense, at balls and evening parties kept near the more solid people, looking listless and superfluous, with a submissive, uninterested expression, as though he had been brought there for sale, who yet believed in his right to be happy, to have children by her; and I kept trying to understand why she had met him first and not me, and why such a terrible mistake in our lives need have happened.

'And when I went to the town I saw every time from her eyes that she was expecting me, and she would confess to me herself that she had had a peculiar feeling all that day and had guessed that I should come. We talked a long time, and were silent, yet we did not confess our love to each other, but timidly and jealously concealed it. We were afraid of everything that might reveal our secret to ourselves. I loved her tenderly, deeply, but I reflected and kept asking myself what our love could lead to if we had not the strength to fight against it. It seemed to be incredible that my gentle, sad love could all at once coarsely break up the even tenor of the life of her husband, her children, and all the household in which I was so loved and trusted. Would it be honourable? She would go away with me, but where? Where could

I take her? It would have been a different matter if I had had a beautiful, interesting life – if, for instance, I had been struggling for the emancipation of my country, or had been a celebrated man of science, an artist or a painter; but as it was it would mean taking her from one everyday humdrum life to another as humdrum or perhaps more so. And how long would our happiness last? What would happen to her in case I was ill, in case I died, or if we simply grew cold to one another?

'And she apparently reasoned in the same way. She thought of her husband, her children, and of her mother, who loved the husband like a son. If she abandoned herself to her feelings she would have to lie, or else to tell the truth, and in her position either would have been equally terrible and inconvenient. And she was tormented by the question whether her love would bring me happiness – would she not complicate my life, which, as it was, was hard enough and full of all sorts of trouble? She fancied she was not young enough for me, that she was not industrious nor energetic enough to begin a new life, and she often talked to her husband of the importance of my marrying a girl of intelligence and merit who would be a capable housewife and a help to me – and she would immediately add that it would be difficult to find such a girl in the whole town.

'Meanwhile the years were passing. Anna Alexyevna already had two children. When I arrived at the Luganovitchs' the servants smiled cordially, the children shouted that Uncle Pavel Konstantinovitch had come, and hung on my neck; everyone was overjoyed. They did not understand what was passing in my soul, and thought that I, too, was happy. Everyone looked on me as a noble being. And grown-ups and children alike felt that a noble being was walking about their rooms, and that gave a peculiar charm to their manner towards me, as though in my presence their life, too, was purer and more beautiful. Anna Alexyevna and I used to go to the theatre together, always walking there; we used to sit side by side in the stalls, our shoulders touching. I would take the opera-glass from her hands without a word, and feel at that minute that she was near me, that she was mine, that we could not live without each other; but by some strange misunderstanding, when we came out of the theatre we always said goodbye and parted as though we were strangers. Goodness knows what people were saying about us in the town already, but there was not a word of truth in it all!

'In the latter years Anna Alexyevna took to going away for frequent visits to her mother or to her sister; she began to suffer from low spirits, she began to recognize that her life was spoilt and unsatisfied, and at times she did not care to see her husband nor her children. She was already being treated for neurasthenia.

'We were silent and still silent, and in the presence of outsiders she displayed a strange irritation in regard to me; whatever I talked about, she disagreed with me, and if I had an argument she sided with my opponent. If I dropped anything, she would say coldly:

'"I congratulate you."

'If I forgot to take the opera-glass when we were going to the theatre, she would say afterwards:

'"I knew you would forget it."

'Luckily or unluckily, there is nothing in our lives that does not end sooner or later. The time of parting came, as Luganovitch was appointed president in one of the western provinces. They had to sell their furniture, their horses, their summer villa. When they drove out to the villa, and afterwards looked back as they were going away, to look for the last time at the garden, at the green roof, everyone was sad, and I realized that I had to say goodbye not only to the villa. It was arranged that at the end of August we should see Anna Alexyevna off to the Crimea, where the doctors were sending her, and that a little later Luganovitch and the children would set off for the western province.

'We were a great crowd to see Anna Alexyevna off. When she had said goodbye to her husband and her children and there was only a minute left before the third bell, I ran into her compartment to put a basket, which she had almost forgotten, on the rack, and I had to say goodbye. When our eyes met in the compartment our spiritual fortitude deserted us both; I took her in my arms, she pressed her face to my breast, and tears flowed from her eyes. Kissing her face, her shoulders, her hands wet with tears – oh, how unhappy we were! – I confessed my love for her, and with a burning pain in my heart I realized how unnecessary, how petty, and how deceptive all that had hindered us from loving was. I understood that when you love you must either, in your reasonings about that love, start from what is highest, from what is more important than happiness or unhappiness, sin or virtue in their accepted meaning, or you must not reason at all.

'I kissed her for the last time, pressed her hand, and parted for ever. The train had already started. I went into the next compartment – it was empty – and until I reached the next station I sat there crying. Then I walked home to Sofino…'

While Alehin was telling his story, the rain left off and the sun came out. Burkin and Ivan Ivanovitch went out on the balcony, from which there was a beautiful view over the garden and the mill-pond, which was shining now in the sunshine like a mirror. They admired it, and at the same time they were sorry that this man with the kind, clever eyes, who had told them this story with such genuine feeling, should be rushing round and round this huge estate like a squirrel on a wheel instead of devoting himself to science or something else which would have made his life more pleasant; and they thought what a sorrowful face Anna Alexyevna must have had when he said goodbye to her in the railway-carriage and kissed her face and shoulders. Both of them had met her in the town, and Burkin knew her and thought her beautiful.

The Lady with a Dog

I

It was said that a new person had appeared on the sea-front: a lady with a little dog. Dmitri Dmitritch Gurov, who had by then been a fortnight at Yalta, and so was fairly at home there, had begun to take an interest in new arrivals. Sitting in Verney's pavilion, he saw, walking on the sea-front, a fair-haired young lady of medium height, wearing a *béret;* a white Pomeranian dog was running behind her.

And afterwards he met her in the public gardens and in the square several times a day. She was walking alone, always wearing the same *béret,* and always with the same white dog; no one knew who she was, and every one called her simply 'the lady with the dog.'

'If she is here alone without a husband or friends, it wouldn't be amiss to make her acquaintance,' Gurov reflected.

He was under forty, but he had a daughter already twelve years old, and two sons at school. He had been married young, when he was a student in his second year, and by now his wife seemed half as old again as he. She was a tall, erect woman with dark eyebrows, staid and dignified, and, as she said of herself, intellectual. She read a great deal, used phonetic spelling, called her husband, not Dmitri, but Dimitri, and she secretly considered him unintelligent, narrow, inelegant, was afraid of her, and did not like to be at home. He had begun being unfaithful to her long ago – had been unfaithful to her often, and, probably on that account, almost always spoke ill of women, and when they were talked about in his presence, used to call them 'the lower race.'

It seemed to him that he had been so schooled by bitter experience that he might call them what he liked, and yet he could not get on for two days together without 'the lower race.' In the society of men he was bored and not himself, with them he was cold and uncommunicative; but when he was in the company of women he felt free, and knew what to say to them and how to behave; and he was at ease with them even when he was silent. In his appearance, in his character, in his whole nature, there was something attractive and elusive which allured women and disposed them in his favour; he knew that, and some force seemed to draw him, too, to them.

Experience often repeated, truly bitter experience, had taught him long ago that with decent people, especially Moscow people – always slow to move and irresolute – every intimacy, which at first so agreeably diversifies life and appears a light and charming adventure, inevitably grows into a regular problem of extreme intricacy, and in the long run the situation becomes unbearable. But at every fresh meeting with an interesting woman this experience seemed to slip out of his memory, and he was eager for life, and everything seemed simple and amusing.

One evening he was dining in the gardens, and the lady in the *béret* came up slowly to take the next table. Her expression, her gait, her dress, and the way she did her hair told him that she was a lady, that she was married, that she was in Yalta for the first time and alone, and that she was dull there... The stories told of the immorality in such places as Yalta are to a great extent untrue; he despised them, and knew that such stories were for the most part made up by persons who would themselves have been glad to sin if they had been able; but when the lady sat down at the next table three paces from him, he remembered these tales of easy conquests, of trips to the mountains, and the tempting thought of a swift, fleeting love affair, a romance with an unknown woman, whose name he did not know, suddenly took possession of him.

He beckoned coaxingly to the Pomeranian, and when the dog came up to him he shook his finger at it. The Pomeranian growled: Gurov shook his finger at it again.

The lady looked at him and at once dropped her eyes.

'He doesn't bite,' she said, and blushed.

'May I give him a bone?' he asked; and when she nodded he asked courteously, 'Have you been long in Yalta?'

'Five days.'

'And I have already dragged out a fortnight here.'

There was a brief silence.

'Time goes fast, and yet it is so dull here!' she said, not looking at him.

'That's only the fashion to say it is dull here. A provincial will live in Belyov or Zhidra and not be dull, and when he comes here it's 'Oh, the dulness! Oh, the dust!' One would think he came from Grenada.'

She laughed. Then both continued eating in silence, like strangers, but after dinner they walked side by side; and there sprang up between them the light jesting conversation of people who are free and satisfied, to whom it does not matter where they go or what they talk about. They walked and talked of the strange light on the sea: the water was of a soft warm lilac hue, and there was a golden streak from the moon upon it. They talked of how sultry it was after a hot day. Gurov told her that he came from Moscow, that he had taken his degree in Arts, but had a post in a bank; that he had trained as an opera-singer, but had given it up, that he owned two houses in Moscow... And from her he learnt that she had grown up in Petersburg, but had lived in S— since her marriage two years before, that she was staying another month in Yalta, and that her husband, who needed a holiday too, might perhaps come and fetch her. She was not sure whether her husband had a post in a Crown Department or under the Provincial Council

– and was amused by her own ignorance. And Gurov learnt, too, that she was called Anna Sergeyevna.

Afterwards he thought about her in his room at the hotel – thought she would certainly meet him next day; it would be sure to happen. As he got into bed he thought how lately she had been a girl at school, doing lessons like his own daughter; he recalled the diffidence, the angularity, that was still manifest in her laugh and her manner of talking with a stranger. This must have been the first time in her life she had been alone in surroundings in which she was followed, looked at, and spoken to merely from a secret motive which she could hardly fail to guess. He recalled her slender, delicate neck, her lovely grey eyes.

'There's something pathetic about her, anyway,' he thought, and fell asleep.

II

A week had passed since they had made acquaintance. It was a holiday. It was sultry indoors, while in the street the wind whirled the dust round and round, and blew people's hats off. It was a thirsty day, and Gurov often went into the pavilion, and pressed Anna Sergeyevna to have syrup and water or an ice. One did not know what to do with oneself.

In the evening when the wind had dropped a little, they went out on the groyne to see the steamer come in. There were a great many people walking about the harbour; they had gathered to welcome someone, bringing bouquets. And two peculiarities of a well-dressed Yalta crowd were very conspicuous: the elderly ladies were dressed like young ones, and there were great numbers of generals.

Owing to the roughness of the sea, the steamer arrived late, after the sun had set, and it was a long time turning about before it reached the groyne. Anna Sergeyevna looked through her lorgnette at the steamer and the passengers as though looking for acquaintances, and when she turned to Gurov her eyes were shining. She talked a great deal and asked disconnected questions, forgetting next moment what she had asked; then she dropped her lorgnette in the crush.

The festive crowd began to disperse; it was too dark to see people's faces. The wind had completely dropped, but Gurov and Anna Sergeyevna still stood as though waiting to see someone else come from the steamer. Anna Sergeyevna was silent now, and sniffed the flowers without looking at Gurov.

'The weather is better this evening,' he said. 'Where shall we go now? Shall we drive somewhere?'

She made no answer.

Then he looked at her intently, and all at once put his arm round her and kissed her on the lips, and breathed in the moisture and the fragrance of the flowers; and he immediately looked round him, anxiously wondering whether anyone had seen them.

'Let us go to your hotel,' he said softly. And both walked quickly.

The room was close and smelt of the scent she had bought at the Japanese shop. Gurov looked at her and thought: 'What different people one meets in the world!' From the past he preserved memories of careless, good-natured women, who loved cheerfully and were grateful to him for the happiness he gave them, however brief it might be; and of women like his wife who loved without any genuine feeling, with superfluous phrases, affectedly, hysterically, with an expression that suggested that it was not love nor passion, but something more significant; and of two or three others, very beautiful, cold women, on whose faces he had caught a glimpse of a rapacious expression – an obstinate desire to snatch from life more than it could give, and these were capricious, unreflecting, domineering, unintelligent women not in their first youth, and when Gurov grew cold to them their beauty excited his hatred, and the lace on their linen seemed to him like scales.

But in this case there was still the diffidence, the angularity of inexperienced youth, an awkward feeling; and there was a sense of consternation as though some one had suddenly knocked at the door. The attitude of Anna Sergeyevna – 'the lady with the dog' – to what had happened was somehow peculiar, very grave, as though it were her fall – so it seemed, and it was strange and inappropriate. Her face dropped and faded, and on both sides of it her long hair hung down mournfully; she mused in a dejected attitude like 'the woman who was a sinner' in an old-fashioned picture.

'It's wrong,' she said. 'You will be the first to despise me now.'

There was a water-melon on the table. Gurov cut himself a slice and began eating it without haste. There followed at least half an hour of silence.

Anna Sergeyevna was touching; there was about her the purity of a good, simple woman who had seen little of life. The solitary candle burning on the table threw a faint light on her face, yet it was clear that she was very unhappy.

'How could I despise you?' asked Gurov. 'You don't know what you are saying.'

'God forgive me,' she said, and her eyes filled with tears. 'It's awful.'

'You seem to feel you need to be forgiven.'

'Forgiven? No. I am a bad, low woman; I despise myself and don't attempt to justify myself. It's not my husband but myself I have deceived. And not only just now; I have been deceiving myself for a long time. My husband may be a good, honest man, but he is a flunkey! I don't know what he does there, what his work is, but I know he is a flunkey! I was twenty when I was married to him. I have been tormented by curiosity; I wanted something better. 'There must be a different sort of life,' I said to myself. I wanted to live! To live, to live! …I was fired by curiosity …you don't understand it, but, I swear to God, I could not control myself; something happened to me: I could not be restrained. I told my husband I was ill, and came here… And here I have been walking about as though I were dazed, like a mad creature; … and now I have become a vulgar, contemptible woman whom any one may despise.'

Gurov felt bored already, listening to her. He was irritated by the naïve tone, by this remorse, so unexpected and inopportune; but for the tears in her eyes, he might have thought she was jesting or playing a part.

'I don't understand,' he said softly. 'What is it you want?'

She hid her face on his breast and pressed close to him.

'Believe me, believe me, I beseech you . . .' she said. 'I love a pure, honest life, and sin is loathsome to me. I don't know what I am doing. Simple people say: 'The Evil One has beguiled me.' And I may say of myself now that the Evil One has beguiled me.'

'Hush, hush!…' he muttered.

He looked at her fixed, scared eyes, kissed her, talked softly and affectionately, and by degrees she was comforted, and her gaiety returned; they both began laughing.

Afterwards when they went out there was not a soul on the sea-front. The town with its cypresses had quite a deathlike air, but the sea still broke noisily on the shore; a single barge was rocking on the waves, and a lantern was blinking sleepily on it.

They found a cab and drove to Oreanda.

'I found out your surname in the hall just now: it was written on the board – Von Diderits,' said Gurov. 'Is your husband a German?'

'No; I believe his grandfather was a German, but he is an Orthodox Russian himself.'

At Oreanda they sat on a seat not far from the church, looked down at the sea, and were silent. Yalta was hardly visible through the morning mist; white clouds stood motionless on the mountain-tops. The leaves did not stir on the trees, grasshoppers chirruped, and the monotonous hollow sound of the sea rising up from below, spoke of the peace, of the eternal sleep awaiting us. So it must have sounded when there was no Yalta, no Oreanda here; so it sounds now, and it will sound as indifferently and monotonously when we are all no more. And in this constancy, in this complete indifference to the life and death of each of us, there lies hid, perhaps, a pledge of our eternal salvation, of the unceasing movement of life upon earth, of unceasing progress towards perfection. Sitting beside a young woman who in the dawn seemed so lovely, soothed and spellbound in these magical surroundings – the sea, mountains, clouds, the open sky – Gurov thought how in reality everything is beautiful in this world when one reflects: everything except what we think or do ourselves when we forget our human dignity and the higher aims of our existence.

A man walked up to them – probably a keeper – looked at them and walked away. And this detail seemed mysterious and beautiful, too. They saw a steamer come from Theodosia, with its lights out in the glow of dawn.

'There is dew on the grass,' said Anna Sergeyevna, after a silence.

'Yes. It's time to go home.'

They went back to the town.

Then they met every day at twelve o'clock on the sea-front, lunched and dined together, went for walks, admired the sea. She complained that she slept badly, that her heart throbbed violently; asked the same questions, troubled now by jealousy and now by the fear that he did not respect her sufficiently. And often in the square or gardens, when there was no one near them, he suddenly drew her to him and kissed her passionately. Complete idleness, these kisses in broad daylight while he looked round in dread of some one's seeing them, the heat, the smell of the sea, and the continual passing to and fro before him of idle, well-dressed, well-fed people, made a new man of him; he told Anna Sergeyevna how beautiful she was, how fascinating. He was impatiently passionate, he would not move a step away from her, while she was often pensive and continually urged him to confess that he did not respect her, did not love her in the least, and thought of her as nothing but a common woman. Rather late almost every evening they drove somewhere out of town, to Oreanda or to the waterfall; and the expedition was always a success, the scenery invariably impressed them as grand and beautiful.

They were expecting her husband to come, but a letter came from him, saying that there was something wrong with his eyes, and he entreated his wife to come home as quickly as possible. Anna Sergeyevna made haste to go.

'It's a good thing I am going away,' she said to Gurov. 'It's the finger of destiny!'

She went by coach and he went with her. They were driving the whole day. When she had got into a compartment of the express, and when the second bell had rung, she said:

'Let me look at you once more… look at you once again. That's right.'

She did not shed tears, but was so sad that she seemed ill, and her face was quivering.

'I shall remember you… think of you,' she said. 'God be with you; be happy. Don't remember evil against me. We are parting forever – it must be so, for we ought never to have met. Well, God be with you.'

The train moved off rapidly, its lights soon vanished from sight, and a minute later there was no sound of it, as though everything had conspired together to end as quickly as possible that sweet delirium, that madness. Left alone on the platform, and gazing into the dark distance, Gurov listened to the chirrup of the grasshoppers and the hum of the telegraph wires, feeling as though he had only just waked up. And he thought, musing, that there had been another episode or adventure in his life, and it, too, was at an end, and nothing was left of it but a memory… He was moved, sad, and conscious of a slight remorse. This young woman whom he would never meet again had not been happy with him; he was genuinely warm and affectionate with her, but yet in his manner, his tone, and his caresses there had been a shade of light irony, the coarse condescension of a happy man who was, besides, almost twice her age. All the time she had called him kind, exceptional, lofty; obviously he had seemed to her different from what he really was, so he had unintentionally deceived her…

Here at the station was already a scent of autumn; it was a cold evening.

'It's time for me to go north,' thought Gurov as he left the platform. 'High time!'

III

At home in Moscow everything was in its winter routine; the stoves were heated, and in the morning it was still dark when the children were having breakfast and getting ready for school, and the nurse would light the lamp for a short time. The frosts had begun already. When the first snow has fallen, on the first day of sledge-driving it is pleasant to see the white earth, the white roofs, to draw soft, delicious breath, and the season brings back the days of one's youth. The old limes and birches, white with hoar-frost, have a good-natured expression; they are nearer to one's heart than cypresses and palms, and near them one doesn't want to be thinking of the sea and the mountains.

Gurov was Moscow born; he arrived in Moscow on a fine frosty day, and when he put on his fur coat and warm gloves, and walked along Petrovka, and when on Saturday evening he heard the ringing of the bells, his recent trip and the places he had seen lost all charm for him. Little by little he became absorbed in Moscow life, greedily read three newspapers a day, and declared he did not read the Moscow papers on principle! He already felt a longing to go to restaurants, clubs, dinner-parties, anniversary celebrations, and he felt flattered at entertaining distinguished lawyers and artists, and at playing cards with a professor at the doctors' club. He could already eat a whole plateful of salt fish and cabbage.

In another month, he fancied, the image of Anna Sergeyevna would be shrouded in a mist in his memory, and only from time to time would visit him in his dreams with a touching smile as others did. But more than a month passed, real winter had come, and everything was still clear in his memory as though he had parted with Anna Sergeyevna only the day before. And his memories glowed more and more vividly. When in the evening stillness he heard from his study the voices of his children, preparing their lessons, or when he listened to a song or the organ at the restaurant, or the storm howled in the chimney, suddenly everything would rise up in his memory: what had happened on the groyne, and the early morning with the mist on the mountains, and the steamer coming from Theodosia, and the kisses. He would pace a long time about his room, remembering it all and smiling; then his memories passed into dreams, and in his fancy the past was mingled with what was to come. Anna Sergeyevna did not visit him in dreams, but followed him about everywhere like a shadow and haunted him. When he shut his eyes he saw her as though she were living before him, and she seemed to him lovelier, younger, tenderer than she was; and he imagined himself finer than he had been in Yalta. In the evenings she peeped out at him from the bookcase, from the fireplace, from the corner – he heard her breathing, the caressing rustle of her dress. In the street he watched the women, looking for someone like her.

He was tormented by an intense desire to confide his memories to someone. But in his home it was impossible to talk of his love, and he had no one outside; he could not talk to his tenants nor to any one at the bank. And what had he to talk of? Had he been in love, then? Had there been anything beautiful, poetical, or edifying or simply

interesting in his relations with Anna Sergeyevna? And there was
nothing for him but to talk vaguely of love, of woman, and no one
guessed what it meant; only his wife twitched her black eyebrows, and
said:

'The part of a lady-killer does not suit you at all, Dimitri.'

One evening, coming out of the doctors' club with an official with
whom he had been playing cards, he could not resist saying:

'If only you knew what a fascinating woman I made the acquaintance of in Yalta!'

The official got into his sledge and was driving away, but turned
suddenly and shouted:

'Dmitri Dmitritch!'

'What?'

'You were right this evening: the sturgeon was a bit too strong!'

These words, so ordinary, for some reason moved Gurov to indignation, and struck him as degrading and unclean. What savage
manners, what people! What senseless nights, what uninteresting,
uneventful days! The rage for card-playing, the gluttony, the drunkenness, the continual talk always about the same thing. Useless pursuits
and conversations always about the same things absorb the better part
of one's time, the better part of one's strength, and in the end there
is left a life grovelling and curtailed, worthless and trivial, and there
is no escaping or getting away from it – just as though one were in a
madhouse or a prison.

Gurov did not sleep all night, and was filled with indignation. And
he had a headache all next day. And the next night he slept badly; he
sat up in bed, thinking, or paced up and down his room. He was sick
of his children, sick of the bank; he had no desire to go anywhere or
to talk of anything.

In the holidays in December he prepared for a journey, and told
his wife he was going to Petersburg to do something in the interests
of a young friend – and he set off for S—. What for? He did not very
well know himself. He wanted to see Anna Sergeyevna and to talk with
her – to arrange a meeting, if possible.

He reached S— in the morning, and took the best room at the
hotel, in which the floor was covered with grey army cloth, and on

the table was an inkstand, grey with dust and adorned with a figure on horseback, with its hat in its hand and its head broken off. The hotel porter gave him the necessary information; Von Diderits lived in a house of his own in Old Gontcharny Street – it was not far from the hotel: he was rich and lived in good style, and had his own horses; everyone in the town knew him. The porter pronounced the name 'Dridirits.'

Gurov went without haste to Old Gontcharny Street and found the house. Just opposite the house stretched a long grey fence adorned with nails.

'One would run away from a fence like that,' thought Gurov, looking from the fence to the windows of the house and back again.

He considered: today was a holiday, and the husband would probably be at home. And in any case it would be tactless to go into the house and upset her. If he were to send her a note it might fall into her husband's hands, and then it might ruin everything. The best thing was to trust to chance. And he kept walking up and down the street by the fence, waiting for the chance. He saw a beggar go in at the gate and dogs fly at him; then an hour later he heard a piano, and the sounds were faint and indistinct. Probably it was Anna Sergeyevna playing. The front door suddenly opened, and an old woman came out, followed by the familiar white Pomeranian. Gurov was on the point of calling to the dog, but his heart began beating violently, and in his excitement he could not remember the dog's name.

He walked up and down, and loathed the grey fence more and more, and by now he thought irritably that Anna Sergeyevna had forgotten him, and was perhaps already amusing herself with someone else, and that that was very natural in a young woman who had nothing to look at from morning till night but that confounded fence. He went back to his hotel room and sat for a long while on the sofa, not knowing what to do, then he had dinner and a long nap.

'How stupid and worrying it is!' he thought when he woke and looked at the dark windows: it was already evening. 'Here I've had a good sleep for some reason. What shall I do in the night?'

He sat on the bed, which was covered by a cheap grey blanket, such as one sees in hospitals, and he taunted himself in his vexation:

'So much for the lady with the dog… so much for the adventure… You're in a nice fix…'

That morning at the station a poster in large letters had caught his eye. 'The Geisha' was to be performed for the first time. He thought of this and went to the theatre.

'It's quite possible she may go to the first performance,' he thought.

The theatre was full. As in all provincial theatres, there was a fog above the chandelier, the gallery was noisy and restless; in the front row the local dandies were standing up before the beginning of the performance, with their hands behind them; in the Governor's box the Governor's daughter, wearing a boa, was sitting in the front seat, while the Governor himself lurked modestly behind the curtain with only his hands visible; the orchestra was a long time tuning up; the stage curtain swayed. All the time the audience were coming in and taking their seats Gurov looked at them eagerly.

Anna Sergeyevna, too, came in. She sat down in the third row, and when Gurov looked at her his heart contracted, and he understood clearly that for him there was in the whole world no creature so near, so precious, and so important to him; she, this little woman, in no way remarkable, lost in a provincial crowd, with a vulgar lorgnette in her hand, filled his whole life now, was his sorrow and his joy, the one happiness that he now desired for himself, and to the sounds of the inferior orchestra, of the wretched provincial violins, he thought how lovely she was. He thought and dreamed.

A young man with small side-whiskers, tall and stooping, came in with Anna Sergeyevna and sat down beside her; he bent his head at every step and seemed to be continually bowing. Most likely this was the husband whom at Yalta, in a rush of bitter feeling, she had called a flunkey. And there really was in his long figure, his side-whiskers, and the small bald patch on his head, something of the flunkey's obsequiousness; his smile was sugary, and in his buttonhole there was some badge of distinction like the number on a waiter.

During the first interval the husband went away to smoke; she remained alone in her stall. Gurov, who was sitting in the stalls, too, went up to her and said in a trembling voice, with a forced smile:

'Good-evening.'

She glanced at him and turned pale, then glanced again with horror, unable to believe her eyes, and tightly gripped the fan and the lorgnette in her hands, evidently struggling with herself not to faint. Both were silent. She was sitting, he was standing, frightened by her confusion and not venturing to sit down beside her. The violins and the flute began tuning up. He felt suddenly frightened; it seemed as though all the people in the boxes were looking at them. She got up and went quickly to the door; he followed her, and both walked senselessly along passages, and up and down stairs, and figures in legal, scholastic, and civil service uniforms, all wearing badges, flitted before their eyes. They caught glimpses of ladies, of fur coats hanging on pegs; the draughts blew on them, bringing a smell of stale tobacco. And Gurov, whose heart was beating violently, thought:

'Oh, heavens! Why are these people here and this orchestra!…'

And at that instant he recalled how when he had seen Anna Sergeyevna off at the station he had thought that everything was over and they would never meet again. But how far they were still from the end!

On the narrow, gloomy staircase over which was written 'To the Amphitheatre,' she stopped.

'How you have frightened me!' she said, breathing hard, still pale and overwhelmed. 'Oh, how you have frightened me! I am half dead. Why have you come? Why?'

'But do understand, Anna, do understand…' he said hastily in a low voice. 'I entreat you to understand…'

She looked at him with dread, with entreaty, with love; she looked at him intently, to keep his features more distinctly in her memory.

'I am so unhappy,' she went on, not heeding him. 'I have thought of nothing but you all the time; I live only in the thought of you. And I wanted to forget, to forget you; but why, oh, why, have you come?'

On the landing above them two schoolboys were smoking and looking down, but that was nothing to Gurov; he drew Anna Sergeyevna to him, and began kissing her face, her cheeks, and her hands.

'What are you doing, what are you doing!' she cried in horror, pushing him away. 'We are mad. Go away today; go away at once… I beseech you by all that is sacred, I implore you… There are people coming this way!'

Someone was coming up the stairs.

'You must go away,' Anna Sergeyevna went on in a whisper. 'Do you hear, Dmitri Dmitritch? I will come and see you in Moscow. I have never been happy; I am miserable now, and I never, never shall be happy, never! Don't make me suffer still more! I swear I'll come to Moscow. But now let us part. My precious, good, dear one, we must part!'

She pressed his hand and began rapidly going downstairs, looking round at him, and from her eyes he could see that she really was unhappy. Gurov stood for a little while, listened, then, when all sound had died away, he found his coat and left the theatre.

IV

And Anna Sergeyevna began coming to see him in Moscow. Once in two or three months she left S——, telling her husband that she was going to consult a doctor about an internal complaint – and her husband believed her, and did not believe her. In Moscow she stayed at the Slaviansky Bazaar hotel, and at once sent a man in a red cap to Gurov. Gurov went to see her, and no one in Moscow knew of it.

Once he was going to see her in this way on a winter morning (the messenger had come the evening before when he was out). With him walked his daughter, whom he wanted to take to school: it was on the way. Snow was falling in big wet flakes.

'It's three degrees above freezing-point, and yet it is snowing,' said Gurov to his daughter. 'The thaw is only on the surface of the earth; there is quite a different temperature at a greater height in the atmosphere.'

'And why are there no thunderstorms in the winter, father?'

He explained that, too. He talked, thinking all the while that he was going to see her, and no living soul knew of it, and probably never would know. He had two lives: one, open, seen and known by all who cared to know, full of relative truth and of relative falsehood, exactly like the lives of his friends and acquaintances; and another life running its course in secret. And through some strange, perhaps accidental, conjunction of circumstances, everything that was essential, of interest and of value to him, everything in which he was sincere and did not deceive himself, everything that made the kernel of his life, was hidden from other people; and all that was false in him, the sheath in which he hid himself to conceal the truth – such, for instance, as his work in the bank, his discussions at the club, his 'lower race', his presence with his wife at anniversary festivities – all that was open. And he judged of others by himself, not believing in what he saw, and always believing that every man had his real, most interesting life under the cover of secrecy and under the cover of night. All personal life rested on secrecy, and possibly it was partly on that account that civilised man was so nervously anxious that personal privacy should be respected.

After leaving his daughter at school, Gurov went on to the Slaviansky Bazaar. He took off his fur coat below, went upstairs, and softly knocked at the door. Anna Sergeyevna, wearing his favourite grey dress, exhausted by the journey and the suspense, had been expecting him since the evening before. She was pale; she looked at him, and did not smile, and he had hardly come in when she fell on his breast. Their kiss was slow and prolonged, as though they had not met for two years.

'Well, how are you getting on there?' he asked. 'What news?'

'Wait; I'll tell you directly… I can't talk.'

She could not speak; she was crying. She turned away from him, and pressed her handkerchief to her eyes.

'Let her have her cry out. I'll sit down and wait,' he thought, and he sat down in an arm-chair.

Then he rang and asked for tea to be brought him, and while he drank his tea she remained standing at the window with her back to him. She was crying from emotion, from the miserable consciousness that their life was so hard for them; they could only meet in secret, hiding themselves from people, like thieves! Was not their life shattered?

'Come, do stop!' he said.

It was evident to him that this love of theirs would not soon be over, that he could not see the end of it. Anna Sergeyevna grew more and more attached to him. She adored him, and it was unthinkable to say to her that it was bound to have an end some day; besides, she would not have believed it!

He went up to her and took her by the shoulders to say something affectionate and cheering, and at that moment he saw himself in the looking-glass.

His hair was already beginning to turn grey. And it seemed strange to him that he had grown so much older, so much plainer during the last few years. The shoulders on which his hands rested were warm and quivering. He felt compassion for this life, still so warm and lovely, but probably already not far from beginning to fade and wither like his own. Why did she love him so much? He always seemed to women different from what he was, and they loved in him not himself, but the man created by their imagination, whom they had been eagerly seeking all their lives; and afterwards, when they noticed their mistake, they loved him all the same. And not one of them had been happy with him. Time passed, he had made their acquaintance, got on with them, parted, but he had never once loved; it was anything you like, but not love.

And only now when his head was grey he had fallen properly, really in love – for the first time in his life.

Anna Sergeyevna and he loved each other like people very close and akin, like husband and wife, like tender friends; it seemed to them that fate itself had meant them for one another, and they could not understand why he had a wife and she a husband; and it was as though they were a pair of birds of passage, caught and forced to live in different cages. They forgave each other for what they were ashamed of in their past, they forgave everything in the present, and felt that this love of theirs had changed them both.

In moments of depression in the past he had comforted himself with any arguments that came into his mind, but now he no longer cared for arguments; he felt profound compassion, he wanted to be sincere and tender…

'Don't cry, my darling,' he said. 'You've had your cry; that's enough… Let us talk now, let us think of some plan.'

Then they spent a long while taking counsel together, talked of how to avoid the necessity for secrecy, for deception, for living in different towns and not seeing each other for long at a time. How could they be free from this intolerable bondage?

'How? How?' he asked, clutching his head. 'How?'

And it seemed as though in a little while the solution would be found, and then a new and splendid life would begin; and it was clear to both of them that they had still a long, long road before them, and that the most complicated and difficult part of it was only just beginning.